D0021170

HIDDEN

HIDDEN

Kelley Armstrong

ILLUSTRATIONS BY ANGILRAM

SUBTERRANEAN PRESS 2011

First Edition

ISBN
978-1-59606-423-2

Subterranean Press
PO Box 190106
Burton, MI 48519

www.subterraneanpress.com

Prologue

"T HERE'S A WOLF in the forest."

Peyton's big sister, Piper, looked up from her homework. "What?"

Peyton pointed at the window. "A wolf. Out there. He was watching me." She tugged one pigtail. "He watches me a lot. I think he's lonely."

Piper scrambled off her chair, put her hand to the glass and cupped it to peer into the darkness.

"He's kinda hard to see," Peyton said. "Because he's black. But he has blue eyes. I can always see his eyes."

Her brother, Pearce, walked in, sneering. "Yeah, a blue-eyed black wolf. She saw a dog, Pipe."

"No, I saw a wolf. He's right—" Peyton pressed her nose to the glass. "He's gone. But it was a wolf. He was really big."

"How big?" Piper asked.

Peyton lifted her hand to the top of her head.

"Uh-huh." Pearce turned to Piper. "Dog. Wolves are smaller than Mrs. Lee's German shepherd. And they're gray with brown eyes. She's a baby, Pipe. She imagines things."

"I'm not a baby! I'm almost five and I go to school."

Piper headed for the door. "I'm going out to take a look."

＊

PIPER HADN'T FOUND any sign of what her sister had seen outside, but it still worried her. Mom didn't pay nearly enough attention to Peyton these days, and she was liable to let her wander into the forest looking for her "wolf." They lived near Algonquin Park. There *were* wolves in their woods—plus bears, porcupines and lynx. Piper tried to watch her little sister, but she was in high school now and couldn't be with her all the time.

She went in to tell Mom what Peyton saw, but Mom was on the phone with Roy, Peyton's dad. They'd split up six months ago. Things had been better with Roy around. A lot better. Kids always whined about their stepdads, but Roy was great. Now he was gone, and Mom was on the phone with him, fighting as usual. He wanted custody of Peyton; Mom wouldn't even let him see her.

Piper had overheard Aunt Nancy saying Mom was doing it to punish Roy. Piper hoped her mom would wake up one day and decide he'd been punished enough. That she'd realize a four-year-old was more than she could handle when she had two jobs and friends and boyfriends. Piper hated being disloyal to her mother, but she secretly hoped that someday Roy would just come and take Peyton. It would be better for everyone. Especially Peyton.

✿

PEYTON STOOD AT her bedroom window and watched the wolf. Peyton had asked her teacher yesterday if wolves could be black, and they'd looked it up on the computer and found pictures of black ones. So Pearce wasn't so smart, even if he was almost twelve.

After that, Peyton dug out the camera Daddy gave her for Christmas. Mommy had gotten mad, saying Peyton was too young for one, but Daddy said he got a good deal on it, and Peyton loved taking pictures. Or she used to, when they'd go into the forest together and find butterflies and hummingbirds. But then Daddy left and Peyton put the camera away. Now she was going to use it to get a photo of the wolf and show Pearce.

She couldn't take pictures through the window. Daddy taught her that. So she tiptoed past Piper's room and slipped into the back hall. Then she put on her coat and boots and went outside.

The wolf was still at the edge of the forest. When she came out, he didn't move, just looked over. She lifted the camera. The wolf backed into the darkness.

Peyton took a few careful steps, until she saw the glow of his blue eyes. She lifted the camera. The wolf moved back. She moved forward. He moved back.

"I just want to take your picture," she said.

He tilted his head, as if listening to her. She raised the camera. He stretched out his front paws, and lowered his head, tail wagging. Then he let out a little yelp, like Mrs. Lee's dog, Baxter, when he wanted to play. As she pushed the camera button, he wheeled and raced off.

Peyton checked the shot, like Daddy showed her. All it showed was the forest and the tip of a black tail.

She sighed. Hearing another yip, she glanced up to see the wolf there. He opened his mouth, tongue hanging out, like he was smiling. When she tried to snap a picture, he dropped and rolled on the ground, so all she got was a blur.

"That's not funny," she said.

He raced around her in a big circle. Then he stopped, right in front of her, and she realized she'd walked into the forest.

She tensed to run, but he just stood there. He lowered his head and flicked his ears. Then he inched closer, head still down, and as big as he was, he didn't seem scary at all. She reached out and patted him. His fur was so thick and soft it was like the coat Aunt Nancy had, with the fur collar, and Peyton only meant to pat his head, but soon she was scratching him behind the ears and burying her fingers in the fur around his neck.

Then he ducked away and danced back. She stepped forward. He stepped back. She laughed. He ran a little ways and she thought she'd scared him off, but he stopped, as if waiting for her.

She glanced over her shoulder at the house. He yipped, and he sounded so lonely and looked so hopeful that she couldn't resist.

"Okay," she said. "Let's play."

He yipped, as if he understood. Then he pretended to run off and they played together, her chasing, him hiding, then jumping out and running. At first, she kept looking back, making sure she could see the lights of the house. But then she forgot, and just kept chasing him.

They'd been playing for a while when he took off and just kept going. She called for him to come back, but he didn't. The game was over. He'd gone home. So should she.

She turned around and peered into the darkness. There were no lights anywhere.

Peyton took a step. Dead leaves crackled under her boots. A moan whispered through the trees and she went still, her heart pounding. It was just branches moving in the wind, that's what Daddy told her. But it had sounded different when he'd been there. Now all she could hear was the wind, making the branches moan and creak, rustling the leaves, whining through the treetops. Then a shriek, right beside her head.

She started to run and tripped. She hit the ground hard. Something jabbed her cheek. She wiped at it and felt blood. Biting back a whimper, she tried to get up, but her foot hurt and she fell again.

She kept trying but it hurt too much. Her foot throbbed and her cheek kept bleeding. And it was cold. So cold and dark and spooky and she was lost and no one would ever find her. That's when she started to cry.

She'd been huddled on the ground for a while when she heard a voice. She sniffed and perked up.

"Hello?" a man called.

She tried to stand, but her foot still wouldn't let her, so she got up on her knees and called back, "I'm here."

Footsteps came toward her. "I thought I heard crying."

"I-I'm lost."

"I see that." The man walked over and the first thing she noticed about him was his blue eyes. They looked just like the wolf's and she blinked. The man smiled and crouched beside her, and she realized he just had regular blue eyes, like Mommy and a lot of other people.

"My name is Peyton James," she said. "I live at 228 Oak Lane."

"Ah. You must be Roy James's little girl."

She nodded.

"I knew your daddy. Come on, then. My place is right over there. I'll get you cleaned up and warmed up and back home to your mommy."

"I can't stand. I hurt my foot."

He bent and looked at it. "Seems like your ankle's twisted. We'll take a better look at it over at my place. I'll carry you there. All right?"

Peyton nodded. He lifted her and she curled up against him, so nice and warm, and let him carry her through the forest.

One

WHEN I PULLED into the lane of our rented Christmas cottage, I was disappointed to see Clay's car wasn't there yet. Not that he'd expected to beat us, but the kids and I had hoped he might. I know he'd hoped so, too. What he'd *really* hoped was to make the drive with us, but he'd been in Montreal at a conference at McGill and when a winter storm hit, it made more sense for him to head straight across to Ontario, rather than loop down to New York State and pick us up.

Kate was out of the car before I even had it in Park. Leaving the door open, she raced into the front yard.

"There's more snow here!" she squealed.

Her twin brother, Logan, pulled on his hat and mitts before following. "No, there isn't. It's the same amount."

"How much is at home?"

"Twenty-seven inches. But we're in Canada now, so it's centimeters. About seventy centimeters."

Kate pointed. "That's more than seventy cent-er-meters."

Logan rolled his eyes at me as I grabbed bags from the back.

"Because it's a drift," he said.

"Then what's that?"

He walked over as she bent to point at something. As soon as he was close enough, she grabbed his jacket and pitched him headfirst into the drift.

"Should have seen that one coming, baby," I said as I walked to the door.

I put down the bags to fumble with the lockbox. Behind me, Logan sat on the drift, grumbling, until Kate made the mistake of thinking he might be serious, went to apologize and found herself lying in the snow beside him.

She should have seen that coming, too. She probably had, same as he did. But if you don't go along with the prank, you lose the right to retaliate.

I left the kids roughhousing in the snow, but didn't close the inside door, so I could hear them. I opened the living room curtains, too, so I could keep an eye on them.

I've read articles about bubble-wrapping your children, and sometimes I think I'm guilty of that. Granted, the twins are only four, but I hadn't been much older than them before I was trekking down to the corner store. Of course, in my case, that was because no one in my foster homes much cared what I did, and most times, whatever danger I encountered on the streets wasn't as ugly as what waited for me inside those homes.

But I do hover too much with the twins. I chalk it up to instinct. Not just maternal, but wolf—as a werewolf, I'm naturally protective.

Finally, when Kate ventured too close to the forest's edge, I stepped onto the porch.

"Paths, Mommy," she said, grinning. "There's lots of paths."

"I know. We'll go exploring as soon as I've unpacked. Just come back into the yard."

Logan gave me that look that has me convinced he's a fourteen-year-old trapped in a four-year-old's body. "We know not to go in the woods, Momma. Kate's just looking. I'm watching her. It seems..." He gazed wistfully into the forest's dark depths. "Nice."

Is Logan a werewolf, too? He should be—it's passed through the male line. Except Clay and I are both bitten werewolves. Either way, it *shouldn't* pass on to Kate. Yet seeing their expressions as they gazed into the forest made me wonder, as I'd been wondering for the past couple of years. Both showed secondary characteristics as well—excellent hearing, excellent reflexes, increased strength. But even with hereditary werewolves that shouldn't happen so young, and really, it was impossible to measure. I told myself it didn't matter. Whatever would be, would be. That was Clay's attitude. I worried a little more. Okay, a lot more.

"See that stump?" I said, pointing. "You can go in that far."

"Thanks, Momma," Logan said. The books say children don't develop the ability to display sarcasm until they're about six, but they also say kids shouldn't be reading fluently—let alone reading reference books—before first grade, meaning whoever wrote them has never met my son.

I stuck out my tongue at him—proving yet again that he doesn't inherit his maturity from me—and went back inside.

I let myself wander past the front rooms, out of sight of the kids, but kept my ears attuned for the first squeal of trouble.

The chalet was gorgeous. Jeremy had picked it out, so I'd expect no less. I didn't want to imagine how much a two-week rental cost. We could afford it, but I still stress over things like that.

Clay and I live with Jeremy. Clay always has—or he has since Jeremy found him as a child werewolf in Louisiana. He brought Clay home and raised him, and when I came into the picture, the household expanded to three.

Well, not exactly. There was a decade in the middle where I'd come and gone, Clay and I locked in an endless war of resentment and betrayal and love.

Clay was the one who'd bitten me, in a panic when he thought Jeremy would separate us. Maybe that sounds like something to be forgiven, but it's not, and for ten years the anger and the hurt and the hate came very easily. The love was tougher to deal with. That's what kept me running until, finally, he changed and I changed, and we resolved to try again. It still wasn't the most serene relationship, but in that way, our children do take after us—they'll bicker and they'll battle, but the only time they're truly miserable is when they're apart.

Occasionally, though, the bickering and battling—and even just the good-natured rambunctious roughhousing—does become a bit much for the other member of our household. So when Jeremy mentioned a chalet for Christmas, Clay suggested we go up a week early, and let Jeremy and the rest of the Pack join us on the twenty-sixth.

It will be our first Christmas with just the four of us. As much as I love Jeremy, I kind of like the idea.

*

I DECIDED THERE was really no need to unpack as soon as we arrived. So I tossed the bags in the bedroom, and carted in the groceries we'd bought in town. Perishables in the fridge, rest left in the bags, granola bars and juice boxes stuffed into a knapsack, then back outside I went.

A white Christmas is never a given. Not at home—just outside Syracuse—and not even here, near Algonquin Park. But it was December twenty-first and we'd had snow for almost a week now, with no sign of a sudden rise in temperature before the holiday.

The twins are still at that age where the first snow of winter is like their first ever. While I'm sure they remembered snow, it seems to be more of a sensory memory, the chill of flakes on their skin, the crunch of the crust under their boots, the sweet clean smell of it. When it started to fall a week ago, they raced outside, and I'd barely been able to get them in since.

Now as I tramped along, they ignored the paths and zoomed through the brush and trees, as if every unbroken expanse was new territory to be conquered.

They zipped out of sight a few times, but I could still hear the swish of their snow-pants, so I didn't call them back. Then they disappeared and everything went silent. I pivoted, trying to catch their scent on the wind, but it was empty. That just meant they were downwind, but my heart started to thump.

"Logan? Kate?"

A purple mitten appeared over a bush. I trekked over to find them crouched, hats off, ears to the snow. They motioned me to silence as I approached.

"Mice," Kate whispered.

I knelt. Even before I put my ear down, I could hear the *skritch-skritch* of mice tunneling under the snow.

"Can you catch one?" Kate asked.

I lifted my brows. "Catch one?"

"Dad can catch them," Logan said.

His eyes glinted with a look I knew well from his father. Challenge. I laughed under my breath.

"Oh, he can, can he?"

I took off one glove. The twins giggled and hunkered down. I put my ear to the snow, listening and waiting. Then—

My hand came up empty. The twins covered their mouths to stifle laughter as I mock-glared at them.

"Dad can't always do it the first time either," Logan said.

"Thank you."

I cleared my throat and made a production of getting into position again. I listened for the patter, then scooped up a squirming mouse. I held it firmly, keeping its teeth away from my bare skin. Those oversized incisors only flashed a couple of times before it got a whiff of my wolf scent and froze.

"Can I hold him?" Kate said.

"Dad lets us if we keep our mitts on and our hand flat."

I put the mouse on Kate's outstretched palm. It cowered there as she lifted it to her face and petted its tiny head.

"It's okay," she crooned. "I'm not going to eat you."

"I wonder what it would taste like?" Logan said.

"Crunchy," Kate said, and they both started giggling.

Which, actually, was true. As wolves, Clay and I would chomp them down like popcorn. Sounds completely revolting when I'm in human form, but that won't stop me from doing it next time we Change.

Logan reached over to touch the mouse, and they talked to it and patted it as if they hadn't just been discussing what it would taste like. I could chalk their comment up to innocent childish curiosity. After all, they certainly didn't see us eating mice. They didn't know we were werewolves.

Kate dug a hole in the snow and carefully lowered the mouse in. As she did, the breeze changed and I caught a scent that had me tensing and lifting my head.

"What do you smell, Mommy?" Kate asked.

"See," Logan said. "What does she *see*."

They exchanged a glance, and for a second, I felt like the child, watching the adults passing a look that said they were humoring me. About a year ago, they'd started noticing when we smelled things. Maybe it was the involuntary flare of our nostrils. Sometimes I admitted it—if it was something that could be reasonably smelled by anyone. The rest of the time, I'd say no, that I'd just heard or seen something.

This was the first time they'd called me on it with that shared look. Clay would say it's a sign that we should tell them. But I argued they were still too young to be burdened with that secret. We just had to be more careful.

"Was it Dad?" Logan asked.

"Hmm?"

"Did you...see Dad?"

Kate shook her head. "No, if it was Daddy, she'd be happy." She slid onto my knee, her arm going around my neck. "She's worried."

I tried not to look startled. I shouldn't be. Our quiet son may be the intellectual prodigy, but our wild daughter was the genius when it came to reading emotions.

I hugged her, burying my face against her blond curls. "I thought I heard a strange noise, but it's gone now. Nothing to worry about."

She studied my expression and nodded. It was true. I had no idea what I'd smelled—it'd been too faint. Just a whiff of something that said "danger," gone before I could seize and decipher it. As I stood, lifting Kate in my arms, I looked around, listening and sniffing. Nothing.

I resisted the urge to herd the kids back inside and we continued exploring the forest. A few minutes later, I caught a scent that I did recognize.

"Daddy!" Kate squealed when she caught me smiling.

She raced to her brother and hit him hard enough to send him flying. Then she grabbed his hand and yanked him to his feet.

"Daddy's here! Let's sneak up on him."

Logan glanced at me. "Momma?"

"Go on."

The kids raced back in the direction of the cabin. I caught a distinct movement to the left. So did they, Kate screeching, then Logan shushing her, as they slipped off in that direction.

I found a stump to sit on and listened. I heard the swish of snow-pants as they tried to sneak up on Clay. Then his laugh when they failed. Their shouts as they tried to catch him. Yelps of frustration when they lost him. Finally, the nearly silent crunch of careful footfalls behind me.

I waited until the footfalls stopped, then dodged to the side as Clay tackled air and stumbled.

"Getting old," I said. "Losing your touch."

"You're losing yours if you didn't take advantage of the chance to knock me into the snow."

"Only because you'd have pulled me down and then we'd have ended up in a place we don't have time to visit, unless you led the kids a lot farther away than I think."

He stepped toward me. "Nah, but there is a nice thicket over there. We could probably hide for a few minutes before they found us."

"But then I'd have to be quiet. It's been a week. It won't be quiet."

He grinned and caught me up in a rib-crushing kiss, one that reminded me that these occasional weeks apart were not necessarily a bad thing.

"Think I can wear them out enough for a nap?" he asked.

"Not their first day here. They're wired."

"Mmm."

He kissed me again. At some point, I thought the ground disappeared from under my feet, but I wasn't really sure until I felt a tree against my back, then his hands on my rear, lifting me up to straddle him. As he pushed against me, I gasped.

"Very nice," I said. "But probably not a good idea considering we have about two minutes before they find us."

He tilted his head, blue eyes glinting. "It's been a week. Two minutes is probably—"

I slapped a hand over his mouth. "No. It's not. I want more. At least five."

He laughed and pulled my hand away, then kissed me again, letting me stay on the ground this time, which helped a bit, but not much. Just the smell of him—the heady scent that had already faded from our bed—was enough to make me think that thicket didn't seem so bad. I could be quiet. Quiet enough, anyway.

"You sure about that nap?" Clay said. "I passed a drugstore in town. Gotta be something there to help them sleep."

I chuckled. "If I honestly believed you'd give your kids cough medicine to make them sleep, I might be tempted. But I think it's going to have to be a shower."

"That'll do." He cocked his head again, and I picked up the faint whisper of snow-pants. He gave me one last smack of a kiss. "Not ideal, but good enough."

"Now you need to go work up a sweat to justify it."

He grinned. "That won't be hard. I think we're about to be—"

Kate let out a war-whoop as she launched herself from the bushes and flew onto Clay's back. He spun around and grabbed Logan as he rushed out. Kate dropped from her perch and grabbed his leg. Clay went down, managing to twist just in time to avoid landing on Logan. The twins piled on as they tried to pin him. There was a flurry of snow and a tangle of arms and legs. Then Kate sailed into a drift, her brother following, and Clay leapt to his feet and ran.

Kate squealed and gave chase. Logan glanced at me. I motioned that we'd slip through the woods and try to cut them off. A blaze of a grin lit up his face. His father's grin. I scooped him up and planted a kiss on top of his head.

"Do you think we can catch them?" he whispered.

"I'm sure we can. And if we can't…" I hefted the knapsack. "Food. We can lay a trap."

Another grin. Then we set out.

TWO

WE CAUGHT CLAY and Kate without resorting to traps. A snowball fight ensued, which started as Logan and me versus them, somehow switched to guys versus girls, and ended up as parents versus kids. We lost. I could say we let them win, but they've been taking archery lessons from Jeremy, and their accuracy has much improved. Also, they've learned that we're fast on the ground, but if they launch an aerial attack from the trees, we're in trouble.

The food came out next. Clay and I didn't get much—the kids declared that first pick went to the victors, which is a Pack-ingrained logic we can't argue with.

As we ate, Kate gave Clay the rundown on our schedule for the next few days. They'd planned it with military precision. Logan even wrote out lists, which made me suspect he'd been spending too much time with Lucas.

Bonfires, tobogganing, hiking, board games, gift wrapping, Christmas baking...they were going to keep us busy. Also, unbeknownst to me, they'd noticed a place in town that rented snowshoes and cross-country skis, so they'd added those activities to the schedule, withholding that information until Daddy arrived because while Mommy would probably say yes, it was a sure bet that Daddy would.

While they chattered, I peered into the woods and was unable to shake the feeling we were being watched. I got up and paced around, trying not to be too obvious about it, but I couldn't find any scent on the breeze. When Clay caught my gaze with arched brows, a slow look around told him something was making me anxious, and he excused himself for a "bathroom" break to do a wider search, but came back with nothing.

"Sorry," I murmured when he returned. "New territory."

"Alpha instincts kicking in," he said. "Can't complain about that."

In a Pack, the Alpha is responsible for the safety of the group. If he's around, everyone else can relax. A couple of years ago, if you'd asked me whether I did that when Jeremy was there, I'd have rolled my eyes and said no. I wasn't like the others. I wasn't raised a werewolf. I didn't share their Pack mentality.

Then Jeremy named me Alpha-elect. Which I could say is an incredible honor, but the truth is that if Clay didn't want the job, there was really no one else. And Clay decidedly did not want the job. He was the ideal beta—second-in-command, Pack enforcer, Alpha's bodyguard. The best fighter around, and happy to keep that as his defining role, leaving the boring politics of leadership to someone else. Namely me.

Only after I became Alpha-elect did I realize how much I *did* relax when Jeremy was around. I'd assimilated the mindset without realizing it.

Now it was up to me. Suddenly, every new scrap of "territory" had to be scouted for danger. I knew Clay would do that—it was his job, and I suspected he'd done a full circle before meeting up with us. But I was hyper-alert, too, and something out here bothered me. Maybe it was because the kids were with us. Maybe it was just that Alpha instinct kicking in, as Clay said—a little too new and a little too raw, sensing danger where none existed. Whatever it was, I breathed easier when we finally headed inside.

*

NEXT ON THE kids' agenda was quiet time, when we were all supposed to enjoy private pursuits. So we set them up in the family room with their hobby bags—books, games and other activities—and announced that we were taking a shower. Together.

Kate sighed. "Are there water problems here, too?"

"We aren't sure yet," I said. "But we are on a well system, just like at home, and you know what happens there. Sometimes it gets a little low."

"But it never runs out," Kate said.

"That's because we conserve it," Clay said.

"We should get it fixed," Logan said, not looking up from his book.

"Uh-uh," Kate said. "No strangers in the house. Mommy and Daddy can just keep sharing showers when it's low."

"That we can." Clay picked her up and tossed her onto the sofa. "Just for you."

THERE WAS A bathroom in the master suite upstairs, but that was too far away from the kids. So we hurried into the back hall. After pushing open three doors and finding a closet and two bedrooms, I think Clay was ready to say screw it and try our luck with a bed instead. The next door was a bath. He pushed me in, and managed to kick it closed, lock it and get me on the counter all seemingly in one motion. Then he set the alarm on his watch for ten minutes—about as much time as we could count on interruption-free.

Clothing came off in a flurry of deep kisses and sharp tugs, laughs and curses when something didn't quite peel as fast as we'd like. Ripping would be easier. But we're kinder to our attire when the kids are around—one too many times having to explain that Mommy's shirt got caught on a branch during her walk with Daddy. And so did his jeans. And the socks? Well, they kind of fell off. Somewhere. Clothing destruction is now reserved for kid-free trips.

I was still pushing off my jeans as Clay pulled me from the counter, kicked open the shower door and swung me inside. My back hit the wall hard enough to leave me wincing at the bang.

"Loud pipes," he murmured.

"Uh-huh. You just better hope they don't come running to investigate."

"That's okay. I'll be done before they get here."

I laughed and wrapped my fingers in his curls, pulling him in for a deep, hungry kiss that served for ten seconds of foreplay before he was inside me. I wasn't complaining. It felt so good. So damned good. Like he'd been gone two months instead of two weeks. The feel of him. The smell of him. The sound of his harsh growls as he thrust.

Clay could joke about being fast, but I'm no better. Foreplay has its place, but not now, not when we'd been separated. It wasn't long before I arched, hissing, biting my lip to keep from crying out. His hands slid up to the back of my head and pulled me down in a kiss, stifling his growls and my gasps as we climaxed.

We stayed there, me still straddling him, panting, noses buried against each other's shoulders. I closed my eyes and inhaled his scent and felt him shudder and sigh, and whisper in my ear, telling me how much he missed me, how much he loved me.

Then his watch beeped. He smacked it off with a soft growl. His hands moved to my hair, entwining it in his fingers as he leaned against my ear again, hot breath tickling.

"They're being quiet. I think we have a few more—"

A rattle at the door. A knock. Kate's voice. "Mommy? Daddy?"

Another growl, this one harsher, swallowed as he rubbed his face, looking abashed.

"Ditto," I murmured as I grabbed the towels we'd draped over the shower door.

A clatter and scrape at the door as Kate poked something into the lock.

"We really need to teach her not to do that," I said.

A sigh. Another abashed look. Jeremy says Clay had every bathroom lock broken at Stonehaven within a month of living there. The concept of privacy is a human one. As a bitten child, Clay had been more wolf than human and the process never seemed to revert. When he got older, he stayed out of bathrooms if the door was closed—usually—but only because he understood that's what we wanted, even if he thought it was a little silly.

We'd taught the twins to knock and wait before entering. It worked with Logan. Kate interpreted it as "knock and wait three seconds before entering" and nothing we said changed that.

At least the knock gave us time to get the towels on before she popped the lock.

"Good, you're done." She scrabbled onto the vanity and started chattering about her book.

As usual, Logan was right behind her. He'd never break into the bathroom, but he never stops her either. Let Kate risk getting in trouble, then slip in innocently behind her.

"It's almost dark," he said. "We need to eat dinner so we can have the bonfire."

Clay scooped up his clothes. "Just let me get dressed, bud. I'll make dinner if you'll help."

Logan nodded, then looked from Clay to me.

"You're not wet," he said.

"Hmm?" I glanced in the mirror to see my hair, still combed and perfectly dry.

We'd forgotten to turn on the shower. Clay and I both whispered a curse at the same time.

"We, uh…" he began.

"Couldn't figure it out," I said, backing into the shower. "The controls are different and…" I fussed and got a trickle of water. "There. You need to turn this part."

"Oh. Huh." Clay stepped back into the bathroom. "We should have that shower then, darling. Just give us ten more minutes, guys—"

"Hurry," Kate said. "I'll wait here."

"Me, too." Logan parked himself on the closed toilet lid.

I looked at Clay. "The shower can wait. We'll need one even more after the bonfire. All that smoke."

"Good idea."

He left, Logan trailing after him. ⌒

Three

*I*N THE SUMMER, the kids expect weekly bonfires, which can be tough when it isn't dark until ten and you really look forward to some adult time before bed. Much easier in the winter. Colder, too, but I'm the only one bothered by that. Like her father, Kate doesn't seem to feel the chill. If Logan does, he never mentions it, just bundles up and snuggles in beside me.

With bonfires comes food. Oh, hell, pretty much every tradition in a werewolf family comes with food. For fires, it's hotdogs and sausages, marshmallows and s'mores. We settle in with our roasting sticks and talk. If it's the whole Pack, the kids stay quiet, as if hoping to convince everyone they're asleep, so they'll hear something they otherwise wouldn't. This time, they were the ones who did the talking.

The topic was school. They'd started pre-kindergarten this past fall, after months of debate. Kindergarten wasn't mandatory, so Clay had been content to let the kids stay home. I thought they could use the social interaction. Logan wanted to go. Kate did not. The solution would seem to be to just send Logan, but even broaching the possibility brought howls from both sides. It was both or none.

Jeremy sided with me on the social interaction issue. We already had the kids in swimming lessons and gymnastics. They went to craft classes, too, which Kate loved. But, really, they needed more.

I'd tried mommy-tot play-dates but…I struggled with the mommy part. I had so little in common with the other women, and hearing stories of their children always made me feel I was screwing up, disciplining too much or not enough, scarring my kids for life because we didn't have pets or stick to a regular bedtime. So I stopped the play-dates and settled for playground visits. With no other kids in the Pack, that meant the twins spent most of their time in the company of adults. More peer interaction was a must. Even Clay reluctantly agreed it would be wise.

Eventually Jeremy was the one who persuaded Kate to go, by stressing kindergarten's emphasis on crafts and music. After the first few days, she'd declared this school stuff wasn't so bad. I think, too, that she enjoyed the academic part. At home, Logan was leaps and bounds ahead of her. Although we praised her, it wasn't until she got to school and compared herself to the other kids that she finally felt smart.

The problem, as it turned out, was Logan. His experience was resurrecting bad memories for Clay. After Jeremy had rescued Clay, he'd been put in kindergarten—at seven years old. He still remembers the horror, being expected to hold hands and sing songs when he thought he'd be studying science and history and math. That's what it's like for Logan. Hearing him at the bonfire—struggling to add to his sister's enthusiastic retellings of classroom adventures—broke my heart.

I leaned against him as he pulled a marshmallow from his stick. "Did I tell you Jeremy and I are going to check out that new school? It's the same one your dad went to. It's a private school, so they can give you special lessons. Harder ones."

"Isn't that the one Dad got kicked out of?"

Clay choked on a s'more.

"Where did you hear that?" I asked.

"Uncle Nick. He was talking to Reese. He said Daddy got kicked out of kindergarten."

"For cutting up the guinea pig!" Kate said, giggling from Clay's lap.

"Dissecting." Logan gave her a stern look. "That's different. It was already dead."

Clay put his arm around Logan's shoulders. "Exactly what I said. But your mom and Jeremy say the school has changed from when I went, which was a while ago."

I grinned. "A long, long, long—"

A handful of snow hit my cheek.

"A while ago," Clay said. "But I've seen the curriculum and it's much better. They'll put you in the right classes. I'll make sure of it."

"And me?" Kate said.

"Extra music lessons," I said. "They have voice coaches, too."

She squealed and jumped on her brother and they went down, rolling like puppies in the snow, until they got a little too close to the fire and we both leapt up to pull them back.

In the commotion, we didn't hear someone approaching. It wasn't until a whiff of scent wafted past that I stiffened and shushed the kids. Clay caught the smell, too, and jumped to his feet.

"What's wrong, Dad?" Logan said.

"Someone's coming." Kate tilted her head and frowned. "It's one of us."

The hair on my neck bristled. It *was* "one of us." Not a Pack member. Not anyone we knew. But a werewolf. His scent told me that. What did Kate mean, though?

The mutt was coming through the woods. We could hear the crunch of snow under his boots now, his shape still hidden by the leaping flames. Clay stood between us and the forest. I resisted the urge to stand at his side and stayed sitting with Kate on my lap and Logan by my shoulder. I put my arm around Logan, but tried to keep it casual. If I look like I'm cowering behind Clay, it sends the message that I'd be easy prey without him. A message most mutts already hope to see.

I used to say I'm the only living female werewolf. I might be. But I've seen enough in the last ten years to be wary of making such a definitive statement. I'll only say I'm the only one we know about. As I said, the gene passes through the male line, meaning a female werewolf must be bitten. If a mutt bites a human, even by accident, he usually makes sure it's fatal. Otherwise, it's an exposure risk. Even if the human escapes, his chances of surviving the transformation are slim. A woman who survives finds herself a target of every male who's dreamed of a mate. Refuse, and she'll be killed. Accept and his rivals won't let them be happy for long.

Such is the life of a female werewolf. Unless she's lucky enough to be taken in by an Alpha who'll help her through the Change, then be adopted by the Pack, and mated to the most feared werewolf on the continent. All that made my life easier, but I'm still hyper-aware of my body language around outside werewolves. I'd much rather face this mutt on my feet, ready to fight. But that would confuse the twins even more.

It took a moment before the man stepped into the fire-light. He looked mid-thirties, which meant—with our slow aging—he'd be a decade older. Dark hair, husky build, beard crystallized with snow. Dressed in a parka, the hood pulled up, his blue eyes the only spark of color.

"You think this is a good idea?" Clay said, his voice a growl.

The man was a few inches taller than Clay, and with that puffy jacket he seemed twice as wide, but he flinched at the growl, gaze dropping, instinctively submissive.

"I, uh, went to the front door. Then I smelled the fire and heard voices."

"And you figured you'd just invite yourself to a bonfire with my *family*."

The emphasis on the last word had the man's gaze skittering to us, but he glanced away quickly.

"I, uh, saw your wife or, uh, I guess she's your ma—"

"Wife."

"Right. I saw her in town with the little ones. I wanted to introduce myself, so you didn't cross my scent—"

A cough from me drowned out the last word. Kate twisted to glare at me for interrupting the drama.

"I wanted you to know I was here," he said. "That's the right thing to do, isn't it? I mean, I've never actually, uh, met another—"

"Clay?" I cut in. "I'm going to take the kids inside."

He nodded, his gaze never leaving the man. Logan protested as I took his arm. Oddly, Kate stayed silent, and gave her brother a look that quieted him better than my shushing. ⌒

Four

HEN WE GOT inside, Logan said, "Why did we have to come in? He was just saying hello."

"Mommy and Daddy don't like him," Kate said. "They don't want him here." She looked up at me as I unwound her scarf. "Is he a bad man?"

"I don't know, baby. He's a stranger. Everyone has to be careful of strangers."

"Even if they're like us?"

Especially if they're like us. I couldn't say that, of course. Couldn't even acknowledge her question because I wasn't sure what she meant or how to deal with it. I had to talk to Clay first. So I finished getting them undressed as I listened to the voices through the door.

"I'm real sorry about that," the man said. "I didn't mean to spook the little ones."

"You didn't. I'd just like you to be very careful what you say around them."

"Oh. Right. Sorry."

"So, let me see if I understand this. You saw Elena with the kids at the store. Bet that was a surprise."

"Yeah. I was in shock at first, thinking I was mistaken. I mean, I didn't think there could be any women. Like I said, I don't know a lot about us. Just what my father told me and my brother."

"So you saw her, all alone with her kids, and you thought you'd pay a visit after dark. See if she needed any company."

"No, I—"

A thump and a gasp. I pushed back the sidelight drape and glanced out. Clay had the mutt by the collar. The guy wasn't making any move to fight, just lifted his hands in surrender. I squelched an instinctive twinge of disgust. The wolf in me might see cowardice, but my human side knew the guy was being smart, not giving Clay any reason to pummel him into the nearest tree. Odd behavior for a werewolf, though. Faced with a challenger, bravado usually overrules brains, at least until the pummeling begins.

"You know who I am, right?" Clay said, pulling the mutt's face down to his.

"N-no, I—"

"Bullshit."

"No. Honestly, I don't. Like I said, it's just me and my brother. I don't know who you are. I'm sorry if I should."

"He's lying," Kate said.

I looked down to see them both peering out the bottom of the window. I yanked them back fast.

"He's lying, Mommy. He knows who Daddy is."

Damn it, they could hear, too.

"All right, then," I heard Clay say. "Let's pretend you don't know and I'll tell you who I am and what I do to—"

I grabbed both kids, one under each arm and hightailed it deeper into the cabin. Only when I couldn't hear Clay's voice did I put them down.

"How does he know Daddy?" Kate asked, as if our conversation hadn't been interrupted.

"Maybe he's run into him before. At a college or a conference."

"Then why's he lying?" she asked.

"I don't know, baby. How about we get a snack, since our bonfire was so rudely interrupted."

She let me steer them into the kitchen, but wasn't distracted. "He's scared."

"Of Daddy? No. They're just having a...disagreement."

"He *should* be scared of Daddy." Her tone was almost defensive. "But he was scared before he even saw him."

"Nervous," Logan said. "He was stuttering. Nervous is the word you want."

She wheeled on him. "I know what nervous means, smarty-pants. People talk like that when they're scared, too, and he was scared. I can tell."

He nodded, a quiet apology that she accepted with a nod of her own. Then she turned to me.

"It's because he's one of us, isn't it."

"I don't know what you mean by that, baby," I said.

I regretted the words as soon as I said them. She could tell I was lying and the hurt in her eyes cut like a dagger.

"I'm sorry," I said, reaching for her.

She backed out of my grasp. "You know what I mean."

"Okay." I hunkered down in front of her. "What do you mean?"

"You *know*."

"I'm not sure I do. Tell me."

She glowered, jaw working as if she was trying to find words. Then she stamped her foot and howled, "You know! You know!" and I realized *she* didn't know. Somehow she understood that the man had a connection to us. Probably the werewolf notes in his scent. But because she didn't know what we were, she couldn't put words to it.

Watching her face redden in frustration, I felt as if I was betraying her. There are two values a Pack wolf places above all others. Loyalty and trust. We tried to teach our children that they knew they could trust us in every way.

Except one. This secret we were keeping.

It was the right thing to do. It was too much for them to process at their age. Too big a burden of secrecy for them to bear. Yet looking at Kate's fury and frustration, I imagined what it would be like when we finally did tell her. Would she look back on all the times we'd evaded her questions—or outright lied—and hate us for it?

"I'm sorry," I said. "I know you're angry, Kate, and I'm really, really sorry."

A scowl. That was all I got. Then she spun and strode to the counter, where I'd set out a bowl of fruit. She grabbed an apple. Logan silently appeared beside her with a juice box. She took it with a grunt of thanks, vented her frustration with a huge chomp on the apple, then stomped to the hall. As she swung out, she collided with her father.

"Hey," he said. "What's wrong?"

I got another scowl. "Nothing," she said, then circled past him and continued down the hall.

I was still crouching where she'd left me. Logan walked over, gave me a hug and a murmured, "She'll be all right, Momma," then followed his sister.

When they were gone, Clay closed the door.

"She said the guy outside is 'one of us,'" I whispered. "But she doesn't know what that means. She just...smells it or senses it. I don't know. She wanted me to explain."

"Ah."

He walked over and took an apple.

"They're too young," I said. "Everyone agrees." A pause as he bit into the apple. "Everyone except you."

"Yep."

"They're four, Clayton," I said, struggling to keep my voice down. "*Four.* I could barely deal with it at twenty-one."

"That was different," he murmured. He put the apple down and came over, arms going around me, as he realized I was shaking. "We're not going to fight about this. If you want to seriously discuss it, okay. But if you just want to convince me that you're right? This is our special Christmas, Elena. We can fight about this anytime. Let's not do it now."

I slumped against him. "I'm sorry. I... She was just so angry and confused, and I felt so...bad."

"You're doing what you think is right. Hell, I'm not sure it isn't. Jeremy agrees with you." He squeezed me. "We can talk about it later. At home. Where the kids won't be left alone to fend for themselves if we kill each other."

I laughed against his shoulder, then took a deep breath and stepped back. "Okay, so what happened outside?"

Clay picked up his apple again, then circled to the door. A deep sniff to reassure himself that the kids weren't poised right outside. He said, voice low, "He stuck to his story. He saw you and the kids in town. He didn't want to spook you, so he got out of your way. Then he found where you were staying and decided to introduce himself, so you'd know there was another werewolf here."

"And you don't buy that."

"No, darling, I don't. He could have followed you to the truck and said a quick hello. Finding out where you're staying? Coming after dark? I don't like it. Damned stupid move if he knows who I am, which makes me think he doesn't."

"He does," I said. "Kate accidently overheard. She says he's lying. He knows who you are."

"Huh." He didn't question Kate's intuition. "Okay, then he's a fucking idiot."

True. Anyone who knew who Clay was—and it was pretty much a given that every werewolf on the continent did—knew that coming after me wouldn't mean a quick, painless death. To protect Jeremy on his ascension to Alpha, Clay had once cut up a trespassing mutt, kept him alive as long as possible, then made sure a second mutt saw the result and distributed the tale, along with Polaroid pictures. Clay had been seventeen. That's the story. The truth is a little more complicated. But...let's just say Clay really hopes those photos have faded to blank frames before our kids are old enough to stumble on one.

Clay did what he thought he had to do. Together with the occasional reminder killing, it's meant that the Pack hasn't had to worry about trespassing mutts for thirty years. It meant, too, that when we're away from home, most still steer clear. So why hadn't this guy?

"He knew you were here," I said. "There's a second car in the driveway. Your scent is all over the place. Even if he missed that, he'd have smelled you when he came around the house. Plenty of time to realize his mistake. So why go through with it?"

"He wasn't looking for a challenge, that's for sure. Guy was so nervous I thought he was going to piss his pants."

"Scared. Kate said he was scared. Did he say anything else?"

"Not much. Small talk. Did we know anyone around here? Were we up for the holidays? Babbling. I shut him down and sent him on his way."

"Not babbling," I said. "Getting answers. Finding out why we're here. If he knows who we are, then he knows one damned good reason why we might be in his hometown."

"Hunting a man-eater."

I nodded. "I'll check the local news archives. See if this place is known for folks walking into the forest and not walking out again."

Five

I TOOK MY LAPTOP and we settled into the living room with the kids. Kate was still annoyed with me. Not angry—no more glowers—but she wasn't bouncing over to snuggle on the couch either. They were both reading on the floor, Logan on his back, deep into the first Harry Potter book, Kate on her stomach flipping through her illustrated children's encyclopedia of myths and legends.

When I saw what she was reading, I'll admit to a dart of panic—thinking she might be looking up werewolves—but she was just working her way through Norse myths, where she'd left off a few days ago. The book fascinated her, and I could say that was a subconscious recognition that her own family belonged in those pages. But there's a more prosaic explanation for her interest—namely, a father who's an anthropologist specializing in ancient religion, legend and folklore. She heard stories of skin-walkers and Egyptian gods before *Goldilocks and the Three Bears.*

Clay started the fire. I pulled out blankets from a box and laid them over the kids. Logan thanked me. Kate acknowledged hers with a nod, not looking up from her book. Clay had brought a stack of anthropology journals he hadn't gotten to this year. With one in hand, he nudged me from my corner of the sofa and plunked down, so I was sitting with my back against him instead. I opened my laptop and set to work researching.

These days, it's easy to find news on the Internet, but I have access to better sources. I'm a journalist. Freelance these days. Being a Canadian living in the States, I've made that my specialty—covering Canadian issues for American publications. I usually stick to small markets, which don't pay a lot, but I can get away with writing pieces based mostly on research, phone calls and e-mail.

In a place this small—the nearest town was barely a thousand people—you'd think it'd be easy to search for local missing persons. But that's the problem. It's too easy, meaning any man-eater living here wouldn't hunt here. He'll drive two hours south to Toronto. Yet if he's a true man-eater, he'd have a hard time controlling the urge if he stumbled across someone in his own woods while he was in wolf form. That's usually how we catch them.

I found five regional cases of missing persons in the past two years. One was a twenty-year-old hiker, found three days later in Algonquin, cold and hungry. Two were seniors who'd wandered away from their caretakers. One was found alive. The second wasn't, but he'd died from exposure, no signs of animal attack. The last two were kids. Children.

That got my attention, heart picking up speed as I read the first report. I told myself it almost certainly had nothing to do with our resident werewolf. Man-eaters know a missing child raises too many alarms.

The first was a seven-year-old boy who'd wandered off from a campground. Like the hiker, he'd been found, cold and hungry. The second was a four-year-old girl who'd disappeared from her home one night. She hadn't been reported missing for almost twenty-four hours, because the girl's mother woke up late, found the child's room empty and presumed her older daughter had taken her to the sitter. The sitter had been just happy to have an apparent day off and never called to check. So it was dinnertime when the mother realized her little girl was gone. The police didn't even have the time to launch a search before the girl's father had called to say he had her and the case was written off as a custody dispute.

"Is that work?"

I looked up to see Kate standing in front of me. I shut the browser.

"Just a little research," I said.

"You're not supposed to be working. It's family time."

"Huh." Clay folded his journal. "Well, then I guess we're both in trouble, because I'm working, too. You're reading. We're reading. I don't think it matters *what* we're reading."

"Yes, it does. You aren't supposed to work on a vacation. You're *always* working."

Clay sputtered a laugh and elbowed me. "She's got a point, darling. We work at least fifteen hours a week."

Kate nodded. "Too much."

"He's teasing you, Kate," Logan said as he sat up. "Most people work a lot more."

"Forty hours a week is normal," I said.

"Uh-uh," Kate said. "That'd be crazy."

"You know Emily and Sarah at school?" Logan said. "That's their babysitter who comes to pick them up. Because their parents work all day."

"Their parents just say that," Kate said. "If I was their mommy, I'd make them go to a sitter, too. All the time."

"I bet half the kids in your class have daycare in the afternoon," I said. "Your parents are just very, very lucky that they can do most of their work at home. When Uncle Nick and Uncle Antonio come, ask how much they work. Uncle Nick works about forty hours a week. Uncle Antonio runs his own business, so he probably does sixty."

"That's crazy!" Kate said.

Clay leaned over and mock-whispered. "I agree."

"When we have quiet time, your dad and I might do a little work," I said. "We like our jobs. But we'll only do it when you're busy. Okay?"

She nodded. I started to reopen my browser.

"Can we play a game now?" she said. "I'm done reading."

Clay glanced at me. I wasn't finished—I needed to go farther back with missing persons reports. But Kate was standing there, her expression wary, having not quite forgiven me for earlier. As much as I wanted to reassure myself that we didn't have a local man-eater, this *was* our vacation.

I closed the laptop and walked to the shelf of board games.

"Can we play—?" Logan began.

"Not Scrabble," Kate said. "You always win. I want—"

"Not Sorry. You don't even try to win. You just like sending other people back to the start."

Kate smiled.

"How about card games?" I said, pulling a few off the shelf. "We have Uno, Pit—"

"Spoons!" they yelled in unison, and grabbed for the regular deck of cards.

"All right, but you know the rule."

Clay slid down to the floor. "Game over at first blood."

"That's right," I said. "Now go grab some spoons."

*

TWO HOURS AND a dozen card games later, the kids were sound asleep in front of the fire, wearing hot chocolate mustaches, with shortbread cookie crumbs scattered like halos around their heads. We knew better than to move them. So I settled back on the couch with Clay and opened my laptop again.

"You know, you work too much," he said. "All the time."

I laughed. "The worst of it? When she says something like that, I actually have two seconds of guilt before I slap myself upside the head. I think we *should* work forty hour weeks for a while, so they see how good they have it."

"Forty hours? That's crazy."

I laughed again and leaned back against him. Yes, we were both in the extremely lucky position of not needing to work. Living with Jeremy meant pooling our resources, and the lion's share came from him—early years of very good investments, followed by a career as an artist whose work now commanded obscene sums of money.

In those dark years after the bite, when I'd been eager to see the worst in Clay, I'd been quick to accuse him of wasting his genius and an expensive PhD, dabbling in his field like an academic dilettante. The truth is that if we needed to work full-time, we'd be screwed. The Pack was our real job. Clay couldn't hold down a tenured position and I couldn't work in an office when we might have to leave at any moment to investigate a potential man-killer or exposure threat. Between our two "jobs," we still probably didn't put in full-time hours, but it was like being a firefighter—we had to be ready to mobilize at a moment's notice.

This particular fire—the mutt—seemed more smoke than flame. I searched missing persons. I searched murders. Nothing. Now I'd need to investigate him and his brother to write up a dossier for our files. Then, if I later noticed a rash of missing persons in Toronto, I'd know whose door to knock on. A minor inconvenience on our Christmas getaway, but it was a job that I couldn't take a vacation from.

I was about to tell Clay it'd be a research case when I did one last search. Death by misadventure. And that's when I found it.

Once I finished reading, I motioned Clay out of the room. I didn't speak until we were in the kitchen with the door closed.

"There was a death here two weeks ago," I said. "College student home for the holidays. He got drunk at a party, wandered into the woods and fell down a ravine. Guy walking his dog found the body the next day."

"Let me guess. It wasn't all there."

I nodded. "Scavenged by canines. Dogs, they think. Or wolves. We're close enough to Algonquin for wolves. It wasn't a missing person case because his parents figured he'd crashed at a friend's place. It wasn't a murder case because the police presumed he died in the fall."

"Autopsy prove that?"

"I don't think they did one. Small-town tragedy just before the holidays. No one's looking too closely."

"It'd explain why our mutt's scared shitless. Chows down on a local kid and two weeks later we show up."

"Do you think he'll bolt?"

Clay shrugged. "Kinda hoping he does. Let us enjoy our holidays, then come back next month and take care of it."

I paced across the kitchen. "Either way, we need to investigate. And we can't do that with the kids here. Goddamn it!"

Clay came up behind me and touched my waist. "We're not sending the kids away, darling. This is our Christmas together. Just the four of us. Like you wanted."

I turned. "I never said—"

"You don't need to. Most times, you're good with the extended-family thing. But Christmas..." He shrugged. "Christmas is different. You think I don't realize that?"

He did. He had from the start. The Pack hadn't really celebrated Christmas before I came along. They did get together and feast and exchange gifts. Sometimes there was even a tree. But there were no gingerbread cookies or mistletoe or stockings by the fire.

Our first year together, when Clay realized I wanted a real Christmas, he'd done what he always did when faced with a human custom he didn't fully understand. He researched it. Then he gave me a perfect holiday.

"This is our Christmas," he said. "Just the four of us. I know you want that and I know you'd never ask for it. So I set one up, and I'm not going to let some mutt spoil it."

"But the kids—"

"—will be fine, because I'm calling Nick and getting him up here with Reese. We have three days left. They'll babysit. We'll investigate. It'll be wrapped up by the twenty-fourth, and if it isn't, it can wait. The guys will go home and come back with Antonio and Noah on the twenty-sixth."

I shook my head. "We can't make them leave for two days. They'll stay. We can do this another year—"

"No, we're doing it this year. They'll go home or find a hotel."

"That's not very nice."

"Nick's used to it. I'll go call him."

✦

ONE OF THE requirements for our Christmas getaway cottage had been a large master bedroom suite with a king-sized bed. Because, despite the fact that the place had five bedrooms, part of a perfect vacation for the twins meant sharing the parental bed, something that was strongly discouraged at home.

So, when I woke up to feel Clay's fingers slide between my legs, I bolted upright. While he'd never try anything with the kids around, he might have forgotten we weren't alone.

"No kids," he murmured, tugging me back down.

"They shouldn't—"

"Do you really think I'd let them wander around a strange house alone, darling? Especially when we've got a mutt nearby?"

I blinked back sleep. "Right. Sorry. So…" More blinking. "Nick."

"Mmm-hmm. A storm was rolling their way, so they decided to outrun it. Just got in." He wrapped his fingers around my leg. "Are you waking up and going downstairs? Or going back to sleep?"

"Are those my only options?"

"They are."

I laughed. "Sleep it is, then."

"Good."

He started tugging me down again. I resisted.

"Is—?"

"The door is locked."

I smiled and sank back down onto the bed. ⌒

Six

E SHOWERED. TOGETHER. Which is always more fun, particularly when you don't need to set an alarm. Then I dressed and went downstairs while Clay shaved. That's a chore I'm sure he'd hoped to skip for a few days, but if we were investigating, he couldn't look as if he'd just stumbled out of the bush. To be honest, Clay could probably stumble out of the bush after a week without even showering, and still get his questions answered, at least by most of the female population, but shaving never hurts.

I found our kitchen had been commandeered by a young man dressed in baggy sweatpants and a tight Columbia University tee, his feet bare, blond hair tousled as if he'd just rolled out of bed himself. Or slept six hours in a car while Nick drove.

"Kids put you to work already?" I asked as Reese came around the center island for a hug.

"They did. Barely got my shoes off before they handed me the pancake recipe."

Reese is one of two young werewolves the Sorrentinos adopted after our Alaskan adventure. I suppose, given that Reese is twenty-one, *adopted* isn't quite the right word. I'd tracked the young Australian to Alaska, trying to warn him that a couple of mutts were after him. Before I could get to him, he'd bumped into two other mutts. They hadn't exactly rolled out the welcome mat. I'd sent Reese to Nick and Antonio to recover from his injuries. They'd persuaded him to stay, working for Antonio and going back to university.

For years, Jeremy and I had tried to bolster the Pack's depleted ranks by recruiting seasoned mutts. An exercise in futility. By that age, they were true lone wolves, uninterested in the social advantages of a Pack. If they did want to join, it's because they were in trouble and needed protection. With Reese, I realized we'd overlooked the best recruiting option—young wolves, those still feeling a pack animal's need for brotherhood.

Reese was an all-around good kid. He'd grown up on a sheep farm in the Outback, raised by a werewolf father and a mother who'd known what her husband and son were, which is extremely rare. Great parents, judging by their son. Both dead now and Reese blamed himself for that. So he came with some serious baggage, but he was coping. He was a smart and loyal team player, which makes him ideal Pack material. And he knows how to cook.

When I offered to help, he refused.

"You guys take a break this morning," he said. "If I need help, I'll enlist that one."

He pointed a wooden spoon and I turned to see another young man, this one seventeen, but looking a couple of years younger. Two inches shorter than my five-ten. Slight build, light brown hair hanging into dark eyes that didn't meet mine, as if unsure of his welcome.

"Noah!" I said as I hugged him.

As always, he hesitated before returning the embrace. At first I'd thought he wasn't comfortable with typically exuberant Pack greetings. But after that hesitation, his return hug was never tentative, and I'd come to realize that no matter how many times he got an enthusiastic greeting, he was surprised by it. Like not meeting my eyes at first. He always seemed braced for the worst, for someone to decide he wasn't worth the trouble and kick him out.

"I'm done with school for the Christmas break, so Nick asked if I wanted to come. I thought he should call first, but he said you'd be asleep."

"And he knows he didn't need to ask. We just didn't think you'd want to waste your holidays playing babysitter."

"It's okay." He looked out the window at the back woods. "Seems like a nice place."

"It is. And the kids will keep you busy. You wouldn't happen to know how to snowshoe, would you?"

A half-smile. "Sure. Dennis and I did it all the time." Dennis was a former Pack member and Noah's grandfather, who'd been murdered before we arrived in Alaska. "I can teach them if you want."

"I want. Speaking of the kiddies…" I looked around. "With Nick, I presume?"

Noah nodded. "In the living room."

❦

I PEEKED IN, saw Nick with the twins, and got my phone. I snapped and sent a couple of photos. Then Kate saw me and shrieked. Logan zoomed past, sister at his heels, both giggling. I stepped into the room and got some more pictures.

Nick Sorrentino. Forty-seven—a year older than Clay. Being a werewolf, he looks more like thirty-five. Despite a night of driving, he was sleek and impeccably dressed, his casual pants and sweater probably worth more than my best cocktail gown. Even the dark stubble on his face seemed a deliberate part of the look—the GQ magazine version of a guy roughing it in the wilderness. All he needed was his usual killer smile, which was absent this morning, possibly because he was tied to a chair.

"That's got to bring back memories," I said.

It was, indeed, a familiar look for Nick. Or so I've heard. As a child werewolf, Clay had loved to practice stalking and his favorite target had been his best friend. To really make it a challenge, though, Clay had to give Nick a reason to run and hide. So Nick often found himself tied to a tree and left in the forest, sometimes forgotten.

"I'm humoring them," Nick said. "They heard us drive in and, apparently, your husband suggested they ambush me."

"I didn't tell them to tie you up, though," Clay drawled as he walked in. "You get a picture for Antonio and Jeremy, darling?"

"Snapped and sent."

"They'll be very amused," Nick said. "Now, if the kids are gone, I'll get out of this before I lose feeling in my wrists. You need to talk to Kate about how tight she ties her ropes."

He lifted his hands behind the chair and his biceps flexed as he tried to snap the rope. It didn't break.

"Been skipping your workouts again?" I said. "Spending more time in the spa than the weight room?"

"Ha-ha. The rope is just a little stronger—" He tried again, neck muscles bulging.

The rope stayed intact.

"Not gonna work," Clay said. "My kids aren't stupid. They tied your hands back-to-back."

He crouched behind Nick and fussed with the knots.

Nick sighed and looked at me as Clay worked. "So, how's your vacation going?"

"Okay," I said. "But no one's tied me up yet."

Clay grinned. "Trip's still young, darling." He stood. "Looks like I'll need to work on knots with the kids. They used a reef, which isn't a bad choice, but a constrictor would have been better." He lifted his head and sniffed. "Is that ham?"

"Ham and blueberry pancakes. On the menu today, and the next three days. Reese is cooking."

"Huh. Better get some before the kids do."

Clay walked out. Nick shook his hands, as if expecting the rope to fall off.

"Do you really think he untied you?" I said. "He was just checking his kids' handiwork."

"Figures. Can you please— Elena? Elena?"

By THE TIME Nick got himself free, the food was gone. He helped himself to mine. I could point out that I wasn't the only one who'd abandoned him, but he knew better than to steal from Clay's plate.

The chalet had a lovely dining room with a table for ten and huge windows overlooking a patch of birdfeeders. Had we been in there, I'm sure we'd have enjoyed the sight of bright red cardinals or blue jays. But we never made it out of the kitchen. We ate leaning against walls, kids perched on the island, everyone talking, the chatter and laughter loud enough to scare any birds from the distant feeders.

"Thank you, Reese," I said as I helped the kids load their plates into the dishwasher. "That was great."

"I see you got a menu all worked out, so I'll cook while I'm here."

"How come you don't offer to do that at home?" Nick said.

"Because you guys can afford to hire someone." He took the menu from the fridge. "Oooh, Christmas cookies." He turned to the kids. "Are we going to bake cookies this afternoon, guys?"

"Yes!" Kate said.

Clay caught my eye and started opening his mouth to tell Reese no. The cookies were part of our tradition—just the four of us—and one of my favorite parts. I cut him off with a shake of my head.

"Except we can't do the gingerbread," Logan said.

Kate nodded. "Gingerbread is Mommy and Daddy's favorite. They have to make those with us."

It took Reese a moment to figure out what Kate had said. As with many four-year-olds, while her parents could understand her easily, others had to take a moment to decipher her speech.

"Ah," he said. "So, gingerbread is Mom and Dad's domain?"

She nodded. "We can do sugar cookies. They're in special shapes, too. We have reindeer and Santa Claus and snowmen."

"But no wombats or Tasmanian devils or kangaroos," I said.

"Kangaroos?" Reese snorted. "Who wants a cookie in the shape of a giant rat?"

"It's a marsupial, not a rodent," Logan said. "I looked it up the last time you said that."

"Well, books aren't always right, mate. They're giant rats. Smart ones that learned to hop on their back legs to convince us they're cute and harmless. Now, Tasmanian devils, we could do. Just cut out cookies to look like Kate—"

Kate squawked and her brother laughed.

"Okay, guys, we're off," I said. "We'll call."

Clay and I tried to slip out. We made it as far as the door before Kate took a flying leap from the counter and zoomed into our path.

"Where're you going?"

"Mom got a call," Logan said as he walked over. "She needs to check out a story here. That's why Uncle Nick came, remember?"

"Right," I said. "So, we'll see you—"

"When?" Now it was Logan.

"We'll be home by dinner."

"Dinner!" Kate said. "You're working all day?"

"No," Clay said. "It's almost lunchtime now. We'll be back before dinner and we'll be here all evening."

Nick walked into the hall and scooped up a child under each arm. "I think I heard someone mention a bonfire and moonlight skiing. We need to pick up skis in town so we'll be all set."

"Snowshoes, too," Noah said as he walked in. "I'm going to teach everyone snowshoeing tonight."

"Then you kids need to rest up, don't you?" Nick said. "Lots of naps."

Normally, they'd screech at that, but they kept glowering at us.

"We'll be as quick as we can," I said.

Nick jerked his chin toward the door, telling us to just leave. He turned, a child still under each arm, and headed toward the kitchen.

"I bet you haven't asked Reese how he lost his fingers yet," Nick said. "I think he's going to tell you the real story this time."

"He never tells the real story," Kate said.

"Then I guess you don't want to hear the latest one?"

A pause, as if they were struggling not to give in, then Logan said, "Was it a kangaroo? With big rat teeth?"

Kate started giggling.

Reese had lost part of the last two fingers on his right hand during his run-in with the mutts in Alaska. That'd been their way of saying hello. When the twins met him, they'd barely gotten past the introductions before Kate asked what happened to his fingers. Jeremy had tried to shush her, but Reese answered with a long, elaborate story involving two grizzly bears and a fish. Ever since, each time they asked him, he'd make up a new story.

Now, as Nick carried them into the kitchen, I heard Reese saying, "A golden eagle. Apparently, he thought they were worms. Bit them right off."

"How did he think they were worms?" Logan asked.

"Well, that was probably my fault. I was out…"

They headed to the family room as Clay and I continued to the front door. I was putting on my boots when I realized Noah had followed us.

"So, when you guys check out this stuff, it's like a murder investigation? Detective work?"

"Part detective," I said. "Part…"

"Thug," Clay finished.

"I was going to say enforcer."

"It's thug work," Clay said. "Elena questions the guy. I encourage him to answer in the only language most mutts understand. But that's only part of the process. The rest is investigating the murder. Talking to folks in town, trying to get answers from the police, the coroner..."

"Cool. Maybe someday I can come along. Learn the ropes. That's part of being Pack, right? Knowing how to handle this stuff."

"It is."

I put on my jacket. Clay nudged me. I followed his gaze to Noah, who was still standing there. Another nudge and meaningful look, and I understood. Noah wanted to come along.

Clay could just invite Noah himself. Or he could take me aside to discuss it. That's what we would have done a year ago. But now I was Alpha-elect and Clay had decided I should take charge in the field, which meant I had to invite Noah on my own.

Of all the things that annoyed me when I joined the Pack, this topped the list. Sure, Jeremy was the leader, but he had a smart Pack of loyal wolves who'd never try to undermine him. So why couldn't they make suggestions? Give advice?

Because that's not how a wolf-brain works. Werewolves want an absolute leader. Jeremy will occasionally open a matter up for discussion, but the final word is his and no one questions it.

Now I'm ready to be that leader...in all cases but one. Clay is my husband. My mate. My partner in every aspect of my life. An imbalance of power there makes me very uncomfortable.

I don't want to rule him any more than I'd want to be ruled by him. So we've come to an agreement. In the field, I'm in charge, but he's free to nudge, like he was doing with Noah.

I was also free to ignore him. Part of me balked at the thought of taking a seventeen-year-old boy on an investigation. We might do things that I'd rather Noah didn't see. But he was nearly an adult and had already seen more than any kid should. This *was* part of Pack life, and as Alpha, it'd be my job to integrate Noah, to teach him, even if it involved things I wished he never needed to learn.

"Do you want to come along?" I asked.

"Can I?" No smile, but his eyes lit up.

"For part of it. We might ask you to stay in the truck for a while."

"That's okay. I'll go tell Nick."

Seven

OUR MUTT'S NAME was Douglas Eaton. He'd offered it to Clay the night before, which was good, because Clay couldn't ask without seeming to take a friendly interest. Pack werewolves can't take a friendly interest in mutts. Another of those harsh wolf realities that seemed draconian to me, until I spent some time around mutts and realized civility was interpreted as weakness. A friendly werewolf is a naïve werewolf. A naïve werewolf is an easy mark.

We didn't have an address for Eaton, but it was easy enough to get. I just took Noah with me into the post office and asked. Said we needed to drop off a present.

The middle-aged clerk dismissed Noah with a glance. She took slightly longer with me. Trying to tell if I looked like I was from "around here" or the city. It makes a difference in small towns. I'm forty-one, though I look more like early thirties. Five-foot-ten. Slender, Jeremy would say. Skinny, I'd say, though the twins had helped me develop some semblance of curves. An athletic build, I suppose. Dressed in worn jeans, a ski jacket and hiking boots. No makeup. White-blond hair tied in a ponytail.

It didn't take long for me to pass her "not a city girl" test. Just a woman and a teenage boy, maybe a nephew or stepson. Neither remotely intimidating. She gave us the address and directions. Even sketched a map on an envelope and wished us a Merry Christmas.

*

IT TOOK A while to get to Eaton's place. As the postal clerk said, "his house was out with the cottages." In other words, in the woods.

The region up here can be divided into two sections. Cottage country and non-cottage country. There are plenty of cottages *in* non-cottage country, of course, but they're the kind of places owned by average folks, passed down through the generations. Places you lend to your buddies and their families, and get a bottle of rye whiskey in return. In other words, not the million-dollar summer homes surrounding every lake. There were no lakes in this area, not good ones anyway. Just cottages in the woods. And these cottages weren't winterized, meaning the roads to them had big signs warning "Not Maintained in Winter."

Luckily, we'd brought the 4x4. Jeremy's truck. It's an SUV, I guess, but Clay and I call it "the truck." We're not really minivan/SUV people. Jeremy isn't either, but we live in a northern climate and since two-thirds of our household is too damned stubborn to drive anything but a car, the job of being a responsible adult falls to Jeremy, as it so often does.

Contrary to what some 4x4 owners think—as evidenced by the sheer number of them in the ditch after every snowstorm—they aren't invincible winter tanks. It was slow going to Eaton's place. We had to follow twin rutted tracks through three feet of snow. More than once it looked like we'd need to get out and push.

"Nick and Antonio getting you out for much winter driving practice?" Clay asked as he maneuvered through another drift. "I know you weren't driving when you lived in Alaska."

"We've done some, but there's nothing like this at their place."

"I'll take you out when you come back after Christmas."

I twisted in the front seat. "If you want a real challenge, have him take you in *his* car."

Noah's smile said he wouldn't mind that at all. Clay drives a BMW M3. Convertible, no less. Jeremy learned decades ago that cars are the one indulgence he can lavish on Clay without complaint. Pre-kids, Clay's tastes leaned toward Porches, but with the children, he needs a four-seater, and he started paying attention to things like safety ratings.

Clay spent the rest of the trip passing on winter-driving tips. If Noah had heard them already, he gave no sign of it, just leaned forward, nodding and asking questions. When he had Clay's attention, he liked to keep it. Fortunately, it wasn't hard to get—Clay's a natural teacher.

"That it?" Clay pointed at a blue metal flag poking from the snow. A six-digit numeral gave the lot's "911 number." Out here, the mail was general delivery, so you needed that number—along with the street name—to give to 911 in the event of an emergency.

"That's it."

It was a short driveway, shoveled nearly down to the dirt, and empty. At the end stood a small cottage. All the windows were dark.

"Doesn't look like anyone's home," Noah said. "What do you do now?"

"Break in," Clay said.

I twisted to look over the seat. "We'll search for information on Eaton, for both the investigation and my dossiers."

"Because you wouldn't find any evidence of man-eating inside," Noah said. "The guy's not going to leave body parts in the freezer."

I was going to agree and leave it at that, but Clay beat me to it. "Never found any in the freezer. With man-eaters, it's not about developing a taste for eating people. There are two ways a werewolf ends up chowing down on humans. One, he's young, like you. New to the Changes. Lets himself get too close to people. Maybe he's hungry. Maybe he's feverish. Maybe he just sees someone running. Instinct takes over, and it doesn't distinguish between humans and deer. It's all prey."

"Which is why I only Change around you guys."

"Right. In a year or so, we'll start having you Change in places where you can smell humans. Then in places where there *are* humans. You'll learn control. Even then, if you let yourself Change when you're hungry and you stumble on someone who runs? Takes a helluva lot of willpower to keep from chasing him. Even experienced werewolves have been known to screw up."

"And if that happens? What do you guys do about it?"

"Same thing we'd do if it was a new kid. Beat the crap out of him. Let him know we're watching. That's usually enough. Mutts are going to mess up. Support system isn't good enough. It's the second kind of man-eater we're worried about. The ones who don't bother learning control because they like the chase. That's what drives them. They eat their prey because they catch it—natural next step. But they don't chase to eat. They chase for fun. That's not wolf. That's human. They're nothing more than killers."

"Serial killers."

"Right. So they don't leave parts in the freezer, but we do find stuff lying around. Sometimes trophies. Sometimes whole bodies. Sometimes only—"

"Time to knock on the door," I said. "If he's home, he's probably seen us sitting out here and bolted."

"Nah. He bolts, we can track. He'd know better. He's not here."

*

CLAY WAS RIGHT. Eaton wasn't home.

"Now, the thing about breaking into a mutt's place is he's going to know you were there," Clay said to Noah as I peered through the windows.

"Because we'll leave scent."

Clay nodded. "So if you don't want him knowing, you can't go in. Most times, though, you go in because you're okay with him knowing. You're trespassing on his turf. It's a challenge. In fact, sometimes, even if we don't want to search the place, we'll break in. Otherwise, he'll smell us at the door and think we didn't enter because we're afraid of him."

"All clear inside," I said. "We'll—"

A howl cut me short. Noah's head jerked up, following the sound. Another howl joined in. Then a third.

"Shit," Noah whispered. "How many are there?"

"Probably about a dozen," I said.

His eyes rounded.

"It's a sled-dog team," I said. "We passed a sign advertising excursions. Sounds like wolves, though, doesn't it?"

"The pitch is different," Clay said. "The rhythm is different too, because they're howling for a different reason. Loneliness. Boredom. If you hear one in the woods, howling for others, it'll sound more like us, so you have to be careful."

Noah nodded.

"Now, back to the break-in. We could search for a key. Could even pick the lock. If we *break* the lock, he has to fix it." Clay opened the screen door and gave the knob a hard twist. It snapped. "Extra inconvenience for the mutt. Shows we're not messing around."

"But knowing how to use picks is a bonus," I said. "Sometimes brute strength just doesn't cut it. Karl will teach you how to pick locks and work with alarm systems."

A hint of a smile. "And you're okay with me learning that? When I've got a juvie record?"

"Sure," Clay said as he opened the cottage door. "You ever get into that shit again? Lotta trees behind Stonehaven. I'll string you up from one."

"And let the crows peck at my corpse?"

"Nah. Doesn't hurt if you're already dead."

Noah only laughed. He didn't doubt the punishment would be severe, but he seemed almost...Relieved, I think, with Clay's honesty. With the absolutes. None of that wishy-washy, "If you screw up, we might get kinda upset." You screw up, you're in shit. It's language wolves understand.

We stepped into the cottage.

"So," Noah said. "How come Karl isn't hanging by his thumbs from a tree somewhere? He's a thief."

"Karl's special," I said.

Clay muttered under his breath about exactly how *special* Karl was. That was the problem with recruiting experienced mutts—you take them as they are. Karl was a jewel thief. He was also a damned good addition to the Pack. A top-notch fighter, and a guy who came with a very valuable set of special skills. I'd known Karl for almost twenty years, long before he joined the Pack. He wasn't the easiest member to deal with, but I could handle him.

"Karl knows what he's doing," I said. "He gets his own set of rules. Which means he's allowed to steal, but if he ever gets caught...?"

"Tree time," Clay said.

"Which you would enjoy *way* too much."

"Only with Karl. Because he's special."

I shook my head and walked farther into the cabin. It was a decent size. Winterized, obviously. Well-kept on the outside and surprisingly nice on the inside, looking more like an urban professional's condo than a wilderness cabin. Two bedrooms, one with a bed, the other used as an office, a large maple desk with a Mac laptop and neat stacks of paper. Bookcases with actual books on them. Leather sofa set. Big-screen TV. Well-equipped kitchen. Food in the fridge, none of it human body parts.

"If his scent wasn't all over this place, I'd think we had the wrong address," I said. "This is nice."

After a quick tour to get the layout, we gave the place a closer inspection. Clay sniffed for "leftovers," checking closets and looking for basement or attic hatches. I went into the office. I thought I'd caught a whiff of someone else in there.

There was a futon across from the desk. When I sniffed it, I picked up the second scent and knew why it'd been tough to separate.

"A relative," I said to Noah, who'd been following me. "A werewolf relative, which means the scent is similar to his. Eaton mentioned a brother. Smells like he slept here, but not last night."

I waved Noah over to sniff for himself while I looked for signs that the brother was more than a casual visitor. I found it in the closet—clothing too small for Eaton. Not a lot, though.

"Is he living here?" I mused aloud for Noah's benefit. "Or just leaving a few things for when he visits? Let's check the bathroom. If he's a semi-permanent resident, we'll find his things in there."

We didn't. Not even a spare toothbrush. There was one of everything, all of it belonging to Eaton.

"So his brother only visits," Noah said. "That could still make him the man-eater, right? Comes to see Eaton, and kills that college guy while he's here."

"Could be. They're both suspects now, meaning we need to dig up everything we can on both of them. We're looking for two things in particular. First, the brother's name and where he lives, so we can search for man-eating cases there. Second, whether Douglas Eaton has business elsewhere or seems to take a lot of trips, anything that might indicate where he could get away with indulging his habit." ⌒

Eight

I SENT NOAH TO search the bedroom. Clay had the living area. I was taking the most likely source of information—right here in Eaton's office.

I figured out his occupation first. There was a shelf of medical books, mostly pharmaceutical. Pens and notepaper advertised the local drugstore. And, to confirm my hunch, a stack of business cards in a drawer said Eaton was the local pharmacist. Probably at work today, which was good to know. We'd need to talk to him, but it was better if we gathered everything we could first.

It was an odd occupation for a mutt. They're a transient bunch. That's our fault mostly. Traditionally, only Pack wolves can hold territory. Even Jeremy admits it's an archaic system, and it had led to serious trouble years ago, when Karl decided he was tired of asking us for territory and joined a revolt against the Pack. I've argued it would be easier to track trouble-makers if we *didn't* keep them on the move. The problem is, like anything else, if you relax the rules, they don't see a kinder, gentler Pack—they see a weak one. So we've been working on ways to grant temporary territory to mutts who've proven themselves worthy.

Historically, the Pack only concerns itself with mutts south of the border. There are only a handful in Canada, with no Pack of their own. I've been monitoring my country, though, so we are enforcing our "no snacking on the humans" law in Canada. Not the territory one, though. Too much territory, too few mutts.

But it was a law we could call upon, if it suited our needs. Here, it could be leverage to throw Eaton off balance when we interrogated him.

I checked Eaton's laptop. It was password protected, which could mean something, but probably didn't. I've never met a mutt yet who blogged about his adventures in man-eating or exchanged support group emails with others who had a taste for human flesh. Being a pharmacist, he probably had confidential patient information on it.

A search through his filing cabinet gave me a lot more. The guy was a meticulous record-keeper. A high school diploma showed he was originally from North Bay, about three hours north of here. There was something in the dossiers about a werewolf living up there with two sons. Probably Eaton's family. I'd have to get Jeremy to take a look.

Eaton had gone to college in Toronto. After that, he moved around, judging by his Records of Employment. I wrote down all the towns, so I could check for bodies, but if I found any, they'd be old. The deed to his cottage was dated twelve years ago. He'd settled here and seemed to be staying. He'd paid off his mortgage years ago and had bought several surrounding properties when the land went up for sale. Expanding his privacy buffer. Smart move.

He drove a 2007 Dodge Ram. Bought used this year, paid cash. I made a note of the vehicle and the license plate number.

"I found something on the brother," Noah said.

I looked up from the desk.

He walked over and put down an open photo album. "This was in the closet."

He'd opened it to one of the last pages. It was dated five years ago, likely when Eaton—like many people—switched to digital. There were a few pictures of him and a guy who had to be his brother. They looked similar, except for size—his brother was a couple of inches shorter and maybe fifty pounds lighter. Noah took the photo from the page and flipped it over. On the back was written "Me and Mark. Trout Lake. July 2004."

"We have a name, then. Excellent. Thanks." I put the photo in my jacket pocket. "For the dossiers, since I doubt he'll willingly supply a more recent shot."

Clay appeared in the doorway.

"Find anything?" I asked.

"Nah. Got a cubbyhole under the floor, but the hatch is in plain view and it seems to be all camping stuff inside. No attic. No smells of decomp anywhere. Even searched the couch. Only found a fishing lure."

He put it on the desk. I picked up the hook. From the other end dangled a couple squares of hammered metal and a small blue feather.

"That's an earring," I said.

He frowned at it. "You sure?"

"Yes."

"Looks like a lure to me, too," Noah said. "Bet it'd work with fish." He stopped smiling. "Wait. An earring? That could be a trophy, right?"

"Possibly," I said. "But a trophy should be kept someplace safe. This was between the sofa cushions, which sounds more like one of the brothers had company." I pocketed the earring. "If it was a local, she might be a good source of information." I stood. "I think we're done here. Time to head to town."

*

"Elena Michaels," I said as I shook the hand of the local physician, Dr. Woolcott, who also served as coroner. "I'm a freelance journalist working on a series of articles on wolf encroachment into human territory. Have you heard of the North American Society for Lupine Relocation?"

The gray-haired man shook his head. Not surprising, since the "society" didn't exist. At least, not as far as I knew.

I continued. "They advocate a clearer delineation between humans and wolves. Namely, forced relocation of wolves living too close to human settlements. They claim that wolf attacks are on the rise and that, contrary to popular belief, wolves do kill people, but the attacks are mislabeled as scavenging. I'm putting together a series to investigate that claim, by looking into cases of canine scavenging near known wolf populations."

He nodded. "The Mitchell boy. Tragic. Very tragic."

He walked to the filing cabinet and pulled out a folder. When he returned to the desk, he hesitated. I prepared to rattle off some of the publications I'd worked for, even provide references if necessary. I had my ID in hand. All very legit, except for the part about writing the story, but that's the beauty of being a freelancer—if I haven't presold the series, the only person "assigning" me the job is myself.

He looked at Noah. "And this is...?"

"Noah. He's interning with me on his school holiday."

"Ah." A grandfatherly smile. "Are you enjoying yourself, son?"

"I am."

"Well, you may not enjoy these photos. They're a little…" He leaned over to me and lowered his voice. "Graphic."

"I won't look," Noah said.

Woolcott thumped him on the back. "Good boy. I know kids these days have probably seen worse in horror movies, but this isn't special effects. Real death can be hard to take, first time you see it."

Nine months ago, Noah had watched his grandfather tortured and murdered. I doubted anything in those photos would be new to him, but his expression was perfectly solemn when he nodded, then retreated to the patient's chair across the room.

Woolcott showed me the photos. Dillon Mitchell had been found at the bottom of a ravine, only a few hundred feet from the house of a friend, where he'd partied the night before. He was discovered by a neighbor taking his dog for an early morning run. Investigation revealed that Dillon had left the party at one-thirty in the morning. Woolcott guessed he'd fallen down the edge of the ravine and died.

"There was trauma to the back of the head. Whether that was the cause of death or…" He glanced at Noah. "Son?"

"I'll step out."

When Noah was gone, Woolcott said, "He may have just been knocked unconscious. There was a lot of bleeding—the scalp was sliced open and if you've ever cut your head, you know what that's like. It's possible that whatever...ate him smelled the blood."

"And the scavenging actually killed him."

He nodded. "I didn't tell the parents that. I was even hoping to spare them the scavenging part, but they insisted on seeing the body. If you do write your article..."

"I won't mention the possibility that he wasn't dead yet."

"He may very well have been. The blow seemed strong enough."

"Did you recover the rock he struck?"

Woolcott shook his head. "He'd been dragged a ways by the scavengers. We found where he'd fallen, from the blood. Lots of rocks. Some had blood on them."

I leafed through the photographs. The boy had definitely been eaten by something. Damage to the stomach— the usual starting point. It hadn't gone much beyond that, which was consistent with a werewolf. Wild animals will eat as much as they can. Whatever ate Dillon Mitchell only took a few bites.

I picked up another photo. Paw prints in the snow.

"Canine," I said.

"Yep."

I flipped through the file. It wasn't just the coroner's report. The police had apparently given him all the scavenging evidence as well.

"I don't see a size for the paw prints," I said.

"Oh, he was big. Over a hundred pounds, I reckon."

In other words, no one had measured the prints. Guessing at the size was extremely unhelpful. There were two kinds of wolves in the Algonquin Park area. Gray wolves and the smaller Eastern Canadian wolves. The latter averages about seventy pounds. The grays are closer to a hundred. Dogs and hybrids can be much bigger. Werewolves are larger still, because we retain our mass when we Change. Without a measurement, I had no idea if this could be one of the Eatons.

"Any hairs found?" I said.

"Nothing obvious." In other words, if there'd been a tuft caught in a tree, they'd have grabbed it, but otherwise, they hadn't looked.

"Only one set of tracks?"

"Hard to tell. The snow was pretty trampled by the time the officers arrived. Some was from the man who found him, and his dog."

Right. The dog. "Any possibility the dog found the body sooner..."

He shook his head. "She's a Lab. The prints were bigger. I know there's not much there to help you, but we really weren't interested in what ate him. Bad enough something did. As for whether it could have been wolves, I've got a theory of my own, and I don't know whether it supports the direction you're leaning."

"I'm not leaning either way. Just collecting data."

"Good, because I think what ate him looks like a wolf, but isn't."

"Sled dogs."

His brows lifted. "Very good."

"I saw that someone around here owns a team."

"That's right. Bobby Walters. Runs his team professionally, and makes extra cash with the tourists when he isn't racing. Bobby's a great guy. Really good with his dogs. But they get away from him every now and them. Damned canine Houdinis, those huskies. And when they get free, they go looking for food. When they're in training, the best way to get them to obey is to hold back on dinner until they've done the work. Meaning if they get loose…"

"They're hungry."

"And they aren't pets. Chow's cheaper, but whenever Bobby can give them meat, he does. Hunters around here shoot more than they want to dress? They take the extra to Bobby. Same with road kill. He pays them, hauls the carcass out back. Dogs do their thing."

Meaning they might have done it with Dillon Mitchell.

NOAH AND I were heading out when Woolcott's nurse stopped us.

"You're investigating the Mitchell boy's death?" she whispered.

I nodded. Didn't clarify the exact nature of my story. Just nodded.

"I have information," she said, leaning forward, gaze tripping around, like she was about to turn in a Mafia kingpin. "Can I speak to you outside?"

"Sure."

"Go around back," she whispered. "I'll come out the rear door."

Nine

WHETHER YOU'RE PLAYING journalist or private eye, there are two common types you encounter. The steely-eyed "I ain't telling you nuthin'" ones and those who can't tell you their story fast enough. Sadly, neither type usually knows anything useful. They just think they do.

I waved to Clay in the truck, giving him the two-minute sign. He nodded.

The nurse was already at the back door. She didn't come out, just opened it and talked, which made me wonder why the hell we couldn't step inside. I suppose this way felt more clandestine to her. To me, it just felt cold. I pulled my jacket up and hunkered down, trying not to stamp my slowly freezing feet with impatience as she gave us Dillon Mitchell's life story. It could be summed up as "he was a good kid." Which is pretty much the same story you'd get in every case like this.

"I think he was murdered," she said finally. "Everyone's saying it was an accident, but I don't believe it. He only had a beer or two, I heard. Not enough to fall off a cliff."

Actually, according to the coroner's report, his blood level had been 0.11, meaning he wasn't plastered, but he'd had more than a couple of beers. Of course his friends at the party were going to claim otherwise—no one wanted to be responsible for letting him leave drunk.

"I think it was that Romero girl. They'd been fighting something awful since he came back from college. She'd been seeing that other guy, and apparently didn't bother to tell Dillon."

"This is Dillon's girlfriend?"

The nurse nodded. "She's doing a victory lap at high school. Grades weren't good enough for college. Poor Dillon comes home and hears she's been spotted with this new guy. She says they're just friends, but I don't think so."

"Who's the new guy?"

"He's not a local. His brother is, and he's bunking down with him while he looks for work."

This sounded familiar. "Do you know his name?"

"Mike, I think. Or maybe Mark. Doug Eaton's his brother. Works at the pharmacy. Such a nice guy. His brother seems like a sweetheart, too. Just got mixed up with the wrong girl."

*

I CALLED CLAY and told him we were going to hike over to the coffee shop. It was a two-block walk through the center of town, which was busy with holiday shoppers. There was some advantage to Noah and me being seen, as I was sure the nurse wasn't going to keep news of this "murder investigation" to herself. If we were seen around town, more witnesses might come forward.

As we walked, I used my phone to search the Internet for "the Romero girl." Lori was her first name, according to the nurse.

"Got a Facebook hit," I said. "Matches for name, town and school."

"Sweet." Noah took the phone as I held it out. He flipped through tagged photos of the girl. "Makes it easy to find someone, huh? That's why I figured you guys wouldn't want me having one. A Facebook profile, I mean."

"Is that a problem? We could figure something out if you really wanted one."

"Nah." He gave me back the phone. "I just tell my friends I don't have time for that shit. Sure, they bitch, but the alternative…" He shrugged and shoved his hands in his pockets. "I don't want to be found. It's not just the probation thing. I'd finish that if I could. I just…I don't want to be found."

When we'd taken Noah from Alaska, there'd been no easy way to do it. We didn't have a custody claim, and he was still on probation. So we just took him. He'd called his mother from Vancouver and said he was with his dad, and wasn't coming back. She didn't care. It just gave her something to tell the police.

We'd gotten him new ID—the Pack has centuries of experience with that. We were claiming he was Antonio's nephew, so Noah had decided to take the Sorrentino name. A few weeks ago, he'd bought a Christmas card for his mother and we'd had Lucas and Paige mail it from Portland. I'd thought he *wanted* to send that card, that he missed his mother. But I realized he only wanted to make sure she knew he was safe and happy, in case any maternal twinges made her consider looking for him.

"You're not going back," I said softly as we turned the corner. "Whatever happens, you don't ever have to go back."

He nodded, gaze on the snow being kicked up by his boots. We passed a middle-aged couple and exchanged Merry Christmases.

"You like being a journalist?" Noah asked.

"I do."

"It seems cool. I'd like the investigating part, but then you have to write the stories, and I'm not good at that. I've been thinking..." More snow kicked. "I might like law enforcement. As a career. But I suppose I can't, with the fake ID and all."

"You'd be surprised," I murmured. "I'm sure we could back up the paper trail enough, if that's what you wanted."

HIDDEN

He shrugged. "I dunno. Everyone says you need to be at least five-foot-ten, and I don't think I'm ever going to get there."

"You've still got time. Besides, there isn't a height restriction in most places these days."

"If I want to investigate, though, I need to be a detective. That means I should have a degree. I don't think I can get one. Hell, it'd be a miracle if I got into college."

"Nick says you're getting good grades."

He looked over at me. "And what kind of grades did Nick get?"

"Um, good enough."

"Which is what I'm getting. I'm passing. For me, that's an improvement. Holding me back a year was a good idea, but it only means I get Cs instead of Ds. I just...I don't do well in school. I understand stuff if I'm doing it, but remembering terms and lists and equations?" He shook his head. "They just don't stick."

When we gave Noah new ID, we'd made him a year younger—sixteen instead of seventeen. We said it was because all the trouble in Alaska put him behind. In truth, he was young for his age, in every way. His father said his mom drank while she was pregnant and Noah had FAE, Fetal Alcohol Effects, which is a less severe form of Fetal Alcohol Syndrome.

I'm not fond of labels. I feel like when you stick one on it glosses over the underlying issue. In my case, I avoid movies

95

or novels about abused kids, because it brings back night-mares. Does it help to call it Post-Traumatic Stress Disorder? Not really. I have issues that I'm still working through and I'm going to keep working through, and that's what matters.

What matters with Noah is helping him cope with his problems. He's easily frustrated and has difficulty concentrating, which really doesn't help in school, but Antonio, Nick and Reese are all working with him, and I'd say that C grades were a marked improvement, for a kid who'd been failing.

I could tell him that. Be supportive and encouraging. But I'd seen Clay with him and I'd seen what worked.

"Do you want to go to college?" I said.

"I don't know."

"Well, that's up to you. If you want it, you're going to need to work for it. You're right. Becoming a cop wouldn't be easy. We'd have to fix your background for security checks. You're a little small, so you'd need to really bump up your workouts with Antonio. He's not a big guy, either, but he's the only one in the Pack who can take on Clay."

"But Antonio's build is different. I'm skinny—"

"And if you can't put in the effort, then you'll stay skinny."

He squared his shoulders. "I can put in the effort."

"Then do that. Same as school. No one expects you to be as strong as Antonio. No one expects you to be as smart as

Clay. Just make the effort. That's the only way you're going to find out if you can get what you want."

A few more steps. Then, "You're right."

"Whew."

He smiled over at me. We walked in silence until I pointed out the coffee shop across the road. As we crossed, he said, "I was thinking of asking Antonio if I could do part-time security at the office. I hate to ask, because I'm not really qualified, so he'd just be giving me a job because I'm his..." He struggled for a word. "Ward. Honorary nephew. Whatever."

"And as his honorary nephew, you're entitled to a job in the family business. It's called networking. You take advantage of every 'in' you have. Ask him. He'll set you up."

"Okay."

We stepped into the coffee shop. It was a Tim Hortons—the chain that seemed to have found its way into every town big enough to support one. Clay sat in the corner by the side exit. That door wasn't shutting properly, and I could feel the draft ten feet away. That explained why Clay had chosen it—it was an unpopular spot. But the corner was no longer as empty as it had probably been when he sat down. A group of young women had taken the table beside his. They were talking loudly, over-doing their excited chatter and laughs, casting glances his way.

"Oh, look," I said as we walked in. "Clay's making friends already. He's such a sociable guy."

Noah grinned. "Does he really not notice those girls? Or is he just pretending he doesn't?"

"He might not. He used to get nasty about it, but he learned that can backfire. Lots of women like a bad boy. Since they're not about to stop noticing him anytime soon, he just stopped noticing them noticing."

"Rough life."

I could say it *was* rough. Clay's uncomfortable with any kind of attention. But no awkward teenage boy wants to hear about the hardships of a middle-aged guy who has twenty-year-old girls drooling over him.

This time, though, I think Clay did notice. Sidelong glances are easy to ignore. A table of giggling girls is not. The second I got inside, his head shot up. He waved us over where two coffees waited, one beside him and one across the table. I started for the one across the table, but he tugged me to his side and gave me a kiss.

"Public displays of affection?" I murmured. "Those girls must really be getting on your nerves."

"They started off talking about how hot older guys are, then moved on to discussions of their favorite sex positions."

"Ooh. Learn anything?"

He growled under his breath and moved me into the seat between him and the girls. I smiled at them. They scowled back and gave me a once-over, with sniffs that said I wasn't worthy.

I took a sip of my coffee, then told Clay what we'd learned. I kept my voice low. That's an advantage to werewolf hearing—we can discuss things in public that we don't want overheard. Noah had to lean forward to listen in. Being young means his secondary powers haven't fully developed. But he could follow the conversation. Or he did until he got distracted by a girl passing the window.

"Uh, Elena?" Noah said.

He nodded toward the door. The girl was coming into the coffee shop now. She wore a cropped leather jacket, boots with three-inch heels and a miniskirt. At least she had on tights to keep her legs warm. I couldn't blame Noah for getting distracted. She was pretty, with long blond hair and—

"Shit," I murmured.

It was Lori Romero.

"Makes it easy, huh?" Noah said.

It would have, if she didn't plunk herself down with the girls beside us.

"Great," I muttered. "They're not going to be eager to chat with me."

"I'd give it a shot, but I'm a little young for them," Noah said. He looked at Clay.

"No," Clay said.

Noah grinned. "Oh, come on. Take one for the team."

"The team will survive."

"But if she's dating Mark Eaton, then we know she likes older guys."

Clay started to growl a response, but I cut him off.

"She *is* dating Mark Eaton," I said. "Check the earrings."

"Fishing lures," Noah said.

"It's not absolute proof," I said. "But she's the only girl there that favors dangling, sparkly earrings, and we know she's rumored to be seeing Mark. Now we need to talk to her."

"Get Reese to do it," Noah said.

When I hesitated, he said, "Yeah, he won't be thrilled, but he'll do it. Might be good for him. Whatever happened in Australia, he's got to get over it and start dating again. Nick says it isn't healthy."

Clay snorted. "He would. Just leave Reese alone. He'll come around." He shot a quick look at the table of girls. "But, yeah, we should bring him to talk to—"

My cell phone ring cut him short. It was Nick.

"Hey," he said. "Just thought you should know, your local mutt stopped by."

"What?"

Clay's head shot up. I pulled the phone from my ear so he could listen in.

"He was playing good neighbor," Nick said. "See how you guys were making out, if you needed directions to local services, suggestions for good hiking spots, recommendations on local attractions…"

"Bastard."

Nick chuckled. "Yeah, I felt like a jerk telling him to get lost. He really did seem like he was being friendly. But over-friendly, if you know what I mean. Kate says he's still scared."

"Kate was there?"

"He brought gifts for the kids. They heard and came running in before Reese could catch them. Guy seemed to want to talk to them. Kate was willing to chat, and isn't too happy with me for sending him packing." A pause. "She said…She said he's one of us. That we should be nicer to him. I'm…not sure if she overheard you guys talking…"

"She didn't. She said that as soon as he came around last night."

"Huh."

"Did she elaborate?"

"Nope. Want me to ask her what she means?"

"Better not. I tried, and it did not go well. I'll explain later."

"Well, this mutt's not making it easy, either. You know what he brought them for gifts?"

"What?"

"Stuffed wolf pups." ⌒

Ten

E PULLED OVER a hundred feet from Eaton's cottage. Through the trees, we could see his pickup in the drive.

I looked back at Noah. "Remember that part where you need to stay in the truck? This is it."

"I know Clay's going to work the guy over."

"But you don't need to see it."

His jaw set. "I've seen worse."

I glanced at Clay. His expression was impassive, but I knew what he wanted.

"Can we have a second?" I asked Clay.

He got out of the truck, and walked into the woods, circling the cottage, as if scouting.

I turned back to Noah. "You may be okay with seeing what Clay does. But he's not okay with you seeing him do it."

"Oh." A pause, as confusion flickered over his face. Then understanding. "Oh."

I lowered my voice more, in case Clay could hear. "What he does works. It keeps the Pack safe. Doesn't mean he likes doing it. No one should like doing that."

"Right. Of course. I didn't mean—"

"I know."

Noah nodded. "Okay. I'm sorry. Tell him—"

I reached back to squeeze his hand. "I don't need to tell him anything. Just stay in the truck. Please. No matter what. Okay?"

"Okay."

I RAPPED ON the door. I could hear Eaton inside. Probably considering his chances of escaping out a window. I was about to knock again when he opened the door. Clay charged, slamming Eaton across the room. The guy was on the floor—Clay on his chest—before he could blink. I stepped in and closed the door behind me.

"What the fuck did you think you were doing?" Clay snarled. "If you've got a death wish, mutt, just take a goddamn gun and blow your brains out in the woods, because I do not have time for this."

"I-I—"

Clay cut him short with a left hook to the jaw that sent blood spraying. "I told you last night to stay the hell away from my family, and what do you do? Come strolling by today like you're the fucking Welcome Wagon. And you come when I'm not at home—"

"I didn't realize that. Your car was there. The truck was gone, but I knew your wife—" His gaze started to dart toward me, then he stopped himself. "I knew she drove the SUV. So I figured it was okay."

"After I *told* you—"

"I wanted to apologize for spooking you."

"You didn't spook—"

"Alarm, I mean. Or, um, catch you off balance. Coming by your place was stupid. An invasion of territory. I get that now. Like I said, I don't know any other werewolves so I don't understand all the rules."

Clay hauled him up and threw him into an armchair. Eaton stayed down. He kept his gaze lowered. Cowardice? Faking submission? Or smart enough to know he didn't want to give Clay an excuse?

Clay glanced at me for orders. A small shake of my head told him to hold off.

I walked between them, letting Eaton know I wasn't hiding behind my mate. "You gave our children wolves. Toy wolves."

"What? No. They're huskies. Dogs. Check the tags. A friend of mine runs a team of sled dogs and I was inviting them—I mean, you two and them—out for a visit. I know normally we can't get near dogs. But these ones have been raised with me around, so they're fine with the werewolf scent, and I thought that might be a treat for your kids. I know when I was growing up, I always found that tough, not being able to be around animals."

When we didn't reply, he said, "Ask your friend at the house. I gave him a pamphlet."

"And you still don't think that was going to piss us off?" Clay asked. "I told you last night that our kids don't know, and you give them toys that look like wolves?"

Eaton protested that the toys had blue eyes and didn't really look like wolves. I said nothing because the truth is that our kids *do* have toy wolves. When they were babies, it'd been something of a joke with our friends—Pack and other super-naturals. We thought it was cute. Even bought a few ourselves. But now, coming from Eaton it seemed like a threat. Leave or I'll tell your kids your secret.

"What do you want to tell us about Dillon Mitchell?" I said.

He hesitated, frowning, as if trying to make the mental shift. Then he went still.

"Yes, we know about the boy," I said. "I saw the autopsy reports. Saw the photos. Saw the paw prints. So a young man dies in the forest, eaten by an oversized canine, and there's a werewolf in town. One who's very nervous having us around."

"N-no. I mean, yes, I'm nervous. I told you, I've never met other werewolves. But I've heard the stories. I know if I bump into one, he's not going to shake my hand and invite me out for a beer. There's one of me and at least four of you. So, yes, that makes me nervous. But I had nothing to do with that boy dying or being eaten. That was scavengers. I'm not a man-eater."

"And your brother?"

His head shot up. "Mark? N-no. He's not even here. He lives in North Bay."

"But he was here when Dillon Mitchell died. We know that. He was seeing Dillon's girlfriend."

Eaton tried to hide a surge of fear, but it was so strong I could smell it.

"No. Not Mark. Our dad raised us right. We don't kill people. We sure as hell don't eat them. I know how this must look, and yes, I knew about Dillon and I was afraid that's why you were here, but it's a complete coincidence. The night Dillon died, I was with my girlfriend, in the next town over. I can give you her name. It's only fifteen kilometers away, so sure, I could have come back and killed Dillon, but that wouldn't make sense. My girlfriend doesn't know what I am, obviously, so I'm not going to come back here, Change for a run, kill a guy, then go back and crawl into bed with her."

Not if Dillon was just a guy he'd bumped into on a run. But if it was murder—if Eaton killed him intentionally—this would provide a decent alibi. Which would make more sense if Eaton had been the one dating Dillon's girlfriend.

"So you were at your girlfriend's, and your brother was here alone?" I said.

A pause.

"We know he was here that night," I said. "You say you weren't. Ergo, he was here alone."

"He might have been with Lori. That's—"

"Dillon's girlfriend. So they were a couple?"

This would seem a simple enough question. Far simpler than being asked about murder and cannibalism. But he hesitated, his jaw working, chewing over a response.

"Yes," he said finally. Tentative agreement. Uncertain. He followed with a firmer, "Yes. They are. I'd rather he was dating someone closer to his own age, but it doesn't seem to be serious. I'm sure they were together that night. Maybe even at the party." A pause. Then, firmer again, "Yes, they would have been at the party. Which means Mark didn't do it."

"I thought you *knew* he didn't do it," I said. "Because he's not a man-eater."

"Of course. But *you* don't know that, so I'm pointing out that it wouldn't make sense for Mark to be at a party with a girl, then sneak out to Change and hunt down her ex-boyfriend."

His logic was flawed. Before the party, Dillon hadn't realized he *was* Lori's ex-boyfriend. That could have led to a fight.
If Mark wanted him out of the picture, he could kill him as a
wolf, which presumably couldn't be traced back to him.

"I want to speak to Mark," I said. "Where is he?"

"He went home to North Bay, like I said."

"Okay. Give me his cell phone number."

"He doesn't have one. Can't afford it."

"His landline, then."

No answer.

"Email address?"

"He's...in the bush. I know that sounds bad, but he does
it all the time. Just packs a bag and heads off for a week or so."

"In the middle of winter?" I said.

"Sure. Camping's fine if you have the right equipment."

"And where is he camping?"

"Somewhere outside North Bay. He doesn't have set spots."

"Of course he doesn't."

I stepped back. Clay shot forward. Eaton tried to scramble
up, but he was too slow. Clay grabbed him by the shirtfront
and slammed him into the wall.

"You say you don't know who we are, but you're full of shit.
We can *smell* the lies. No matter how isolated you are, you
have some contact with other werewolves. Every mutt does.
It's a matter of survival. There's exactly one female werewolf

out there. Not hard to figure it out who she is, which means you know who I am, too."

"I-I wasn't sure…"

"Bullshit. Who am I?"

Eaton didn't answer. Clay plowed his fist into Eaton's stomach. Eaton gasped, eyes rolling.

"Try again. Who am I?"

"Clayton Danvers."

"And who's she?"

"Elena Michaels. I mean, Dan—"

"Michaels," Clay said. "So you know who we are. Now tell me what we do. Who does Elena speak for?"

"The Alpha. She speaks for the Alpha. You two enforce the will of the Alpha. You keep the Laws of the Pack. You hunt man-eaters."

"And what do we do when we find them?"

He swallowed. "You kill them."

"No." I stepped forward. "For a first-time offender, we remind him of the Law. We show him why it's not wise to break the Law. It's a painful lesson, but there's no permanent damage until the second lesson. There is no third lesson. By that point, it's clear the problem isn't one the werewolf wishes to resolve."

Was that standard procedure in every instance? No. There wasn't a rule book. Every case was different. But those were the basic stages we followed.

I took another step, close enough to see sweat beading on Eaton's broad forehead. "If your brother confesses to accidentally killing and eating Dillon Mitchell, he'll get the first lesson. However, if he refuses to come forward, I'll need to dig deeper to find him, which may turn up more cases and make us decide that he's passed the point of warnings."

"I don't know where he is."

"Yes, you do. You have twenty-four hours to get him and call us. Understood?"

Eaton nodded.

❦

WE RETURNED TO Noah and moved the truck to an empty cottage a half-kilometer away. Then Noah and I hiked back. I was certain Eaton knew where his brother was, and pretty sure he was the one hiding him. So we hoped to catch him going to check on him. But he didn't. We waited for an hour—swapping spots halfway so I could warm up—then Nick called to say Reese was almost done cooking and the kids were simmering themselves, watching the clock. We headed back.

❦

WE FOUND DINNER on the table. Everyone was just settling in. When Kate and Logan didn't greet us at the door, I told myself they were just hungry. Parents can't compete with food. When we walked into the dining room and neither looked up, I knew trouble was brewing.

"That man came over today," Logan said before I could sit down. "He brought us a present."

"So I heard," I said.

Logan pulled his toy from his lap and set it on the table. "It's a Siberian husky."

"No," Kate said. "It's a wolf."

Logan shook his head. "The tag says they're huskies. And they have blue eyes." He pointed at the bright blue beads. "Wolves can't have blue eyes."

"They can if they're babies."

"Your sister's right," Clay said. "Wolves can have blue eyes when they're first born. But Logan's right, too. Those are huskies."

"Logan's is a husky. Mine's a wolf."

I smiled and bent to stroke her curls as I passed. "All right. Yours is a wolf. Do you have a name for her yet?"

She looked up. Her gaze met mine. I could feel it searching, and I struggled to hold it, to keep smiling.

"Why are we being mean to the man, Mommy?" she asked.

"We aren't—"

"Uncle Nick was mean to him. Uncle Nick's never mean to anybody."

I glanced across the table. Nick looked at me helplessly.

"I don't think he meant to be mean," I said carefully. "But the man is a stranger and we don't like strangers giving gifts to our children. You know the rule. We don't take anything from strangers."

"But he's not a stranger. He's one of us."

"She has a point," Reese said from down the table. "You really should be nicer to a fellow Canadian, Elena. Aren't you guys supposed to be nice all the time?"

I made a face at him.

He leaned toward Kate and mock-whispered. "I think your mom's been down in the States too long. She's getting rude, like your dad. Then she comes up here, and a fellow Canadian is just being friendly and she gets all suspicious, because in the States, no one is friendly."

"Uncle Nick is."

"Uncle Nick's weird."

Nick shot back and they continued on, the others joining in, successfully distracting the twins. At least for now. ⌒

Eleven

AFTER DINNER, EVERYONE cleaned up for Reese, then left him prepping pancake batter for the morning. They went outside. I stayed with Reese.

"Thanks for rescuing me," I said.

"No worries. They're smart little guys. That's good in some ways." He took down the flour. "And a pain in the arse in others."

"No kidding." I walked to the fridge, poured myself a glass of water and handed him a bottle of beer.

He checked the label and let out a sigh of relief. "Not American. Thank you."

He popped the top and chugged half the bottle.

"I was wondering something," I said. "How old were you when you found out you were a werewolf? If you don't mind talking about it."

I knew what had happened in Australia. I was the only one Reese had told. Clay knew he'd told me—we don't keep secrets—but he'd never ask for the details. He was just glad that someone knew.

Reese's parents had been killed by the Australian Pack. It was an old grudge. Every Pack is different and it seems the Australian one fit into the "gang of thugs" category. His parents had been hiding since before he was born, and when they were found, it was through Reese. Not his fault. But he blamed himself. So I raised the subject of his youth—and, by extension, his parents—as little as possible.

"It's getting easier," he said. "Never going to be easy, but if I won't talk about them?" He shrugged. "Doesn't seem right. Not what they'd want."

"No, I'm sure it isn't."

He took another long draw on the bottle, then measured the baking powder before continuing.

"I don't remember them telling me. Maybe I always knew or maybe I was so little that I don't remember finding out. It was just…part of who we were. Dad could Change into a wolf. And he could hear me if I snuck out of bed at night or find my scent all over the kitchen if I'd raided the refrigerator, so there was no use lying about it. That was normal life for me."

That's what Clay had wanted. Don't make a big production out of it. Just let them grow up with it as part of their lives. I couldn't believe he'd suggest such a thing. Let *toddlers* know their parents Changed into wolves? We'd have to police every encounter with non-supernaturals until they were old enough to understand why it was a secret.

"And you never let something slip? To the kids next door or down the street?"

He lifted his brows. "Remember where I grew up?"

"Right. Sheep farm. The Outback. No kids next door."

"Sure there were. If by 'next door' you mean the farm ten kilometers over. By the time I was old enough to visit on my own, I was practically old enough to Change. Sure, I had playtime with other kids. My parents made sure I didn't grow up a completely antisocial little heathen. They'd drive me to town twice a week for footy from the time I was old enough to kick a ball. Dad was always there, in case I stuffed up."

"But you never did."

"Sure I did. When I was about three, Mom took me to the zoo and I was watching the wolves and informed a lady that my dad could turn into one of those. She called the cops. They sent scientists to kidnap and study him..."

"Right. Let me guess: she patted you on the head and told your mother you had a vivid imagination."

"Nah, she gave her shit for letting me watch horror movies. Then, when I was five, I was watching cartoons at a family friend's place. There was a wolfman and I said that wasn't a proper werewolf and tried to tell the other kids what a proper werewolf was."

"And your dad stopped you?"

"Nope. He let me finish, then explained the difference between folklore werewolves and movie werewolves. Both times, though, I caught hell when I got home. Got a long lecture plus a double-helping of chores around the farm. I learned my lesson."

He finished his beer, then covered the dry pancake mix with plastic wrap. "You thinking of telling the kids?"

"I… They're so young."

"They are. And you don't live on the Outback. Your kids are in school already. My parents never had to worry about that, with me being home-schooled." He grabbed another beer from the fridge. "You coming outside?"

I nodded.

He grinned. "Good. I told the kids we were going to sabotage Nick's snowshoes. We'll need you to distract him while we work."

SNOWSHOE LESSONS FROM Noah. A hike through the woods with the kids, Reese and I keeping our snowshoes on, Nick abandoning his halfway through after landing in one too many snowdrifts, Clay doing the same…possibly because Nick wasn't the only victim of snowshoe sabotage.

Nick didn't figure it out. Clay did. I landed in a snow-bank of my own. Kids piled on. Snowball fight ensued. Bonfire back at the cottage. No interruptions. No unanswerable questions. Kate snuggled up on my lap at the fire and Logan sat with his dad, deep in a discussion I was too sleepy to follow.

The kids' good mood continued to bedtime. We let them stay up with the adults, then put them down after midnight. The kids brought their toy dogs and as they settled in, Kate put hers on her chest, staring at it. I tensed and glanced at Clay. He shook his head, in answer to my unasked question. Don't try to distract her. Just wait and deal with whatever was coming.

"The man said his friend has sled dogs," Logan said. "He invited us to come see them. Kate said dogs don't like us, but he said these ones like all kids."

"They won't bite or run away," Kate said. "He promised."

"That's a hard thing to promise," Clay said.

Logan nodded. "But we could try, couldn't we? He says they're close by. We can play with the dogs and, if we want, we can take a sled ride."

Kate looked at me and asked, "Can we?" with none of her usual imperiousness. She feared what the answer would be. Sensed it, I think.

"We'll see," Clay said.

She nodded. Admittedly, a "we'll see" from me was often Mom-speak for "Probably not, but I don't want to disappoint you and I'm hoping if I delay an answer, you'll forget the question." From Clay, it really did mean we'd consider it.

"I'm not sure it will work out," Clay said. "But if Mr. Eaton's offer still stands after Christmas, we'll take you over."

An honest answer. Both children nodded. And that was it. No anger. No more questions. They curled up between us with their stuffed dogs and fell asleep.

Which should have been a relief. They were already abandoning the fight. If I kept up this course of action— avoid questions, distract when I could, maneuver out when I couldn't—they'd forget.

Would Kate really forget, though? Or just give up?

When they finally did learn the truth, would she remember this? Of course she would. She wasn't a baby. She'd remember and she'd be furious, rightfully so.

Clay would back me up and pretend it was a mutual decision. Present a united front—that was our tenet of parenting. He'd take a share of Kate's resentment and anger, which wasn't fair so I'd have to admit that he'd wanted them to know all along.

Okay, so Kate would be angry, probably Logan, too, but how deep a betrayal was it? We can pretend we're honest with

our kids, but we aren't. Not really. We tell them stories about Santa Claus, and we know they'll be upset when they learn the truth, but we hope they'll look back and see the magic we added to their childhood.

Clay and I had never considered forgoing the Santa myth. He'd never had it himself. When he was bitten, there was no place for jolly gift-bringing elves in his new reality. There hadn't been much Santa in my life, either—my first Christmas in a foster home, an older foster brother told me the truth. Yet I'd never considered not perpetuating the legend with my own children.

So we did lie. We lied to bring magic to their lives and we lied to protect them. When we finally told Logan and Kate the truth about what we were, would they understand my reasons? Or would they only understand that I'd lied? That Kate had trusted me...and I'd failed.

I could fix this. I could tell them the truth. Yet at the very thought of it, my gut twisted and my brain shrieked. I'd made the right decision. The kids were too young for the truth. I just had to weather this storm.

And yet...

I couldn't sleep. I lay there long after the kids had drifted off and Clay had joined them. Then I eased out of bed and headed for the door, but I could hear Reese and Noah, still down in the family room, talking in front of the fire.

Only one place to go. I pulled on a sweater and the thick, woolen socks Clay had discarded. Then I slipped out onto the balcony overlooking the back woods. ⌒

Twelve

I STOOD THERE, TORN between wanting to make a decision and not wanting to rush the wrong one, not when I was distracted by other problems. This was so damned important.

The more I thought about it, the farther I got from a decision, which only infuriated the hell out of me. Any day now Jeremy could say, "I'm stepping down. You're Alpha." What kind of Alpha would I make if I was freezing my ass off at two a.m., unable to reach a decision on a parenting issue? An Alpha had to be decisive, damn it. An Alpha had to say, "This is my decision" in a way that convinced every Pack wolf that there was no other option.

So what the hell was Jeremy even thinking naming me Alpha? I *always* had doubts. There was no black and white in my world. There were a thousand shades of gray, a thousand permutations for every decision, a thousand possibilities for every choice. You want someone who can make an absolute decision and stand by it, damn the consequences? You want Clay. And if Clay has other qualities not befitting an Alpha, then you make it a joint position. I'd suggested it. Jeremy said no. Clay said no. One wolf to rule them all. That's how it'd always been and how it always would be.

When a warm body pressed against my back, I jumped. Clay's arms tightened around me and he pulled me against him.

"You're freezing, darling. I'm the one who doesn't feel the cold, remember? Come back inside."

"Soon."

A soft sigh. The heat vanished as Clay stepped away and I had to fight the urge to back against him again, tell him to stay. He retreated inside. A moment later, he returned, and moved up behind me again, pulling a comforter around us, his body so blissfully warm that I closed my eyes, everything else sliding away.

"Hear the wolves?" he murmured.

I lifted my head and picked up the distant howling of a wolf pack, miles away.

"If you didn't hear that, you really are thinking hard."

"Worrying," I said.

"Thinking."

I smiled and leaned against him.

"She'll be all right," he said. "They both will. We'll fix this mutt problem, the kids will move on and we'll return to our regularly scheduled Christmas getaway."

I turned in his arms. "I'm starting to wonder if you were right."

He paused. "I'd say I must be dreaming, but you don't seem in the mood for jokes."

"I think we should have told them from the start. Made it part of their lives. We should have discussed it more. I should have listened more."

"We talked plenty. You listened. Honestly? I wasn't completely convinced that my view was right. If I was, I'd have fought for it."

"You did."

He lifted his brows. "If I really thought it was the absolute best thing for our kids, you'd have had a battle on your hands. That was just debate."

"With chair-throwing."

"Heated debate. Fights involve chair-breaking. Chair-throwing is just getting your attention."

"Ah."

He pulled me closer. "There's no perfect answer. I was working from the basis that assimilation into a culture is easier if it's introduced from birth. But the kids *have* been assimilated from birth. They're treated like werewolves. They live like werewolves. They just don't understand the rationale behind it. It's like…" He paused. "Like growing up in a society with ancestor worship, and you do all the rituals and celebrate the holidays, but the 'why' isn't explained until you're old enough to really understand it."

"And you're okay with that?"

"I'm not thrilled with waiting, but it isn't as if you and Jeremy said we had to pretend to be a normal human family for them. Then I'd have fought like hell. If they'd known we were werewolves from the start, the only real advantage is that you wouldn't be on this balcony, freezing your ass off, wondering when is the right time to tell them. The disadvantage is that it's an exposure risk."

"Which is minimal, when you really think about it. No one's going to believe four-year-olds who claim their parents turn into wolves. The real exposure risk comes when they're old enough to Change. I mean, *if* they…"

I trailed off.

"That's the real problem, isn't it?" Clay said.

I looked up at him.

"You're right about the exposure risk," he said. "Hell, I think you just parroted my own words back to me. The true risk comes when a werewolf begins his Changes. When he can throw a classmate into a wall and kill him. When he can start shape-shifting in the middle of a party. But by then, they *have* to know. The real reason you don't want to tell them? Because we don't know if they're ever going to Change. You've heard Nick and Reese talk about what it's like, hitting their teens, the excitement, the anticipation. It's like waiting to be old enough to drive or to drink, multiplied by ten. Everyone warns you it'll be painful as hell, but you don't care. You're finally going to be able to turn into a wolf. You're finally going to join the Pack."

He paused. I turned to listen to the wild wolves and felt tears prickle.

Clay lowered his voice. "And for our kids, that might not happen. That's what you're afraid of. Bringing them up in a life they might never fully share."

"I think..." I paused, gathered my thoughts. "They smell like werewolves. They seem to be showing secondary powers. But that's..."

"Different."

I nodded. "Their smell is different. They're showing powers years before they should and I...I want to see that as proof that they'll be able to Change. Which, in some ways, is crazy. Life would be easier if they couldn't. Take the secondary powers. Leave the pain of the Change. Leave the constant struggle for control. Leave the risk that someday, you're going to lose that battle and look down to see a person, a dead human being—"

I choked. Clay hugged me so tight I couldn't breathe. I squeezed my eyes shut and tried not to remember those days in Toronto, when I'd run from Jeremy, when the Change was still a fever-blind blackout. When I'd woken up to see what I'd done.

"I don't *ever* want our children to go through that," I said. "So I should be happy if they don't Change. But I'm not, because I know how important it will be to them. I know that in spite of the risks, I'd never give up..."

I couldn't finish that. I've reached peace with what Clay did, but that admission is too much. Too exculpatory.

"You wouldn't give up being a werewolf," he murmured. "You just wish it'd happened another way."

I nodded.

Another bone-cracking squeeze. "So do I, darling. More than anything."

I rested my cheek against his chest. The wolves had gone silent now, so I listened to the thump of his heart.

After a moment, he said, "It should have gone the way I planned. Let you know what I was. If, at some point, you wanted to join that part of my life..."

I would have. I know that now. It wouldn't have been a quick decision, but the time would have come when I'd have wanted to share that with him, wanted to experience it for myself, realized it would complete me. And that's exactly what

I was afraid of with our children. That they would realize this was what they needed to complete their lives, and that they'd never be happy without it.

"I think…" I cleared my throat, moved back, started again. "I think Logan will be all right. I think he'll Change. It's Kate I'm worried about. What if she doesn't? Or if he does and she doesn't?" I shook my head. "Maybe I'm being silly. She's only four. She won't be the same person when she's old enough to realize it won't happen. Maybe she'd be okay with it."

He said nothing.

I met his gaze. "She won't, will she?"

He still said nothing, as if even he couldn't put a voice to that fear, that our daughter would not be okay with it.

"She'd want to be bitten," I said. "She'd want us to…" I couldn't finish. After a minute, I said, "Yes, that's what I'm afraid of. That's why I don't want to tell her any sooner than I have to. We can tell her it won't happen for her, hope it will be a surprise if it does, but that won't matter. She'll think it will and when it doesn't, she'll want it. She'll come to us and she'll ask, and if we say no…" I forced myself to met his eyes. "I'm afraid we'd lose her."

A pause. Then, "That's a lot of ifs."

I let out a short laugh. "Worrying about worst-case scenarios? That's not like me at all, is it?"

His turn to laugh. "Okay, so let's work it through. Worst-case scenario. Kate grows up expecting to change into a wolf. Logan does. She doesn't. She asks us to bite her. We say no— it's too dangerous. She hates us forever because we're standing between her and happiness." He stopped. Looked me squarely in the eye. "Only that's not true, is it? If we say no..."

"She can go to someone else," I whispered. "A mutt."

"I can hope our daughter would be smart enough not to let some random mutt bite her. But could she con a mutt into it? Maybe even a Pack member? Reese, Noah... Her brother? We could say no all we want, Elena. That wouldn't stop it from happening. And it won't matter if we tell her now or in a few years. She's still going to want it. All we can hope is that it won't be an issue—she *will* Change. And if she doesn't? We're going to need a game plan...in sixteen years, when we're certain it's not going to happen on its own."

"So there's no sense stressing about it now."

"Right."

I exhaled. "Which brings back the original question. When do we tell them?"

"I'm okay with telling them now. I'm okay with telling them in a year, two, three, even four. More than that? I have a problem. So, you have four years. When you're ready, we'll figure out how we're going to do it. And anytime you want to talk about it?"

"I know where to find you."

"You got it."

I put my arms around his neck. "Thank you."

He arched his brows. "For making myself available to discuss a parenting issue with the mother of my children?"

"No. For knowing what was really worrying me, even when I wasn't sure myself."

I kissed him. His hands slid under my t-shirt, fingers hot against my skin. He hoisted me onto the railing.

"Feel sturdy enough?" he said.

"It's not a long fall."

He laughed and reached to shake the railing. When it didn't budge, he murmured "good," and pulled the comforter around us again.

As we kissed, a shadow moved against the balcony doors. "I think we have company," I murmured.

He turned as Logan cupped his hands against the glass and peered out. He spotted us and waved. I hopped off the railing. Clay opened the door, and whispered, "Hey, bud, you want to come out?"

Logan nodded. Clay lifted him and shut the door quietly, then swiped snow off a chair. He sat, Logan on his knee, tugged me onto his other knee and wrapped the comforter around us.

"Warm enough?" he asked.

Logan nodded.

Clay leaned over to his ear and whispered. "Listen. Do you hear that?"

Logan cocked his head. His eyes widened. "Wolves?"

Clay nodded.

Logan stared out at the sky, listening so intently, with this wistful look on his face, and I could tell myself I was imagining it, but I knew I wasn't. He might not understand what he felt, but when he listened to those wolves, he felt something.

Everyone said Kate was so obviously her father's daughter. Our friends teased Jeremy that it must be like having Clay all over again. Jeremy would smile and nod, but he'd told me that Clay had been more like Logan, serious and quiet, even when he was cutting up the classroom guinea pig and tying Nick to trees. The boisterous energy came later, but there was still that quiet side of him, and I could see it now, as he rested his chin on his son's head, looking out into the night, listening to the wolves.

I twisted sideways, laid my cheek against Clay's shoulder and watched them until I drifted off to sleep. ⌒

Thirteen

WHEN I OPENED my eyes, Kate was crouched on the bed, her face a few inches from mine, staring at me as if she could will me to wake up.

I blinked and yawned.

"Uncle Nick and Reese are up," she whispered.

I glanced at Logan, sitting beside her. Behind him, Clay was sound asleep.

I nodded, "Go on."

Once they'd left, I padded to the door and locked it. Then I reached under the bed to retrieve something I'd stowed there the day before. The next maneuver was tricky, but Clay was so soundly asleep that I managed it with barely a hitch in his breathing.

When I was done, I tugged back the covers. He didn't notice the sudden draft and kept sleeping.

He'd worn sweatpants to bed, for the sake of the kids, but his chest was bare and he was lying on his back, arms over his head. It was a very nice image. Being Pack enforcer means Clay is in amazing shape. He has to be—he doesn't have the natural advantage of size, like some werewolves. Average height, average build. Above-average body. Perfectly toned biceps, muscled back and chest, flat stomach.

When we'd take the twins to parent-tot swimming lessons, Clay would walk out of the changing room, and mothers who'd gawked at him clothed would almost fall into the pool. But when they took a closer look, the frowns would come, the confusion and concern. Then the questions. Is your husband a war vet? Was he in an accident? Because, as perfect as Clay's body appeared, on closer look, it wasn't. On closer look, you saw the scars. Decades-old white ones. Pinkish newer ones. Pits and divots, from chunks ripped out in wolf fights. And on his right arm, the ruts of missing tissue, cut out after an infection that left the limb forever weakened.

The overall damage isn't disfiguring, but on an otherwise jaw-dropping guy, it's discomfiting. Women look at that map of scars and they're horrified. I look at it, and I see his life story. I can trace every scar with my eyes closed. I know where each one came from. A few are even from me. Some friendly fire, some not.

I have scars, too. Not nearly as many, but enough that I used to be uncomfortable in a bathing suit. I've gotten over it.

They're part of my life story, too. Who I am. Who I've chosen to be.

I leaned over Clay now, the tips of my hair tickling his chest, my fingers running across a few of those old scars, remembering. But that wasn't what I was here for, so I pushed the memories aside and settled for admiring the image, then touching him, tasting him, testing exactly how soundly asleep he was. When I flicked my tongue over his nipples, he groaned softly, but didn't wake. Very soundly asleep. Good.

I carefully tugged down his sweatpants and boxers. Then I set about waking him up. It took a few minutes. The soft groans slowly deepened to a delicious growl, a sound more felt than heard, vibrating through him. Finally, a gasp. His eyes opened. He chuckled. He tried to reach for me. Then he grunted in surprise.

I lifted my head. He was arching back to look at the rope binding his wrists to the headboard. He gave an experimental tug. Then his fingers slid to the knots.

"Do they pass muster?" I said. "I used a constrictor knot, like you suggested."

He looked down at me, lips curving in a sleepy grin. He flexed his fingers, motioning for me to come up.

I shook my head. "I'm good. And since you're stuck, I can do what I want. And what I want to do," I lowered my head. "is finish what I started. Acceptable?"

"Don't have much say in the matter, do I?"

"Tragic."

"It is." He grinned, thumped back on the pillows and let me continue.

WE SPENT THE morning with the kids. I did cheat a bit, skipping a morning walk to "do a few things around the house." Clay bustled the twins off before they could protest. I did tidy up, but spent most of the time on my laptop. Research on the Eatons and on disappearances in North Bay, nothing much turning up on either.

I called Jeremy. He shared my opinion of the situation. There was definitely something going on with the Eaton brothers. Likely Mark was the culprit and his big brother was hiding him.

Jeremy shared my risk assessment, too. Minimal. Eaton knew there were four adult werewolves here. He wouldn't risk a strike against us. If Mark was a man-eater, the chances he'd kill again soon were small.

Given all that, Jeremy also seemed to share Clay's hope—that the Eatons would bolt, and we could relax, enjoy our Christmas, and take care of them in the new year. Jeremy couldn't say that, of course. Man-eating was a serious offense that we had to pursue with full vigor. But he made it clear that if the Eatons ran, chasing them would be a waste of time until we had more information.

He also agreed that taking the morning off was fine. I'd seeded my journalist story. Relax, let that spread, and see what came of it. Honestly? I didn't expect anything to come of it and I don't think Jeremy did, either, but he let me have the excuse.

We talked about the kids, too. About Kate's questions. Jeremy listened and said little. Part of that was transitioning me to Alphahood, when he'd still be there to give advice when asked, but not offering it. Part of it was just his general approach to the rearing of our children. He played a huge role in their lives, but Clay and I were their parents. We made the parenting decisions.

Instead I asked questions about children in the Pack, the process of telling them, and the Pack's history with it. What had gone wrong? How had the Pack dealt with it? I didn't ask for his opinion or advice. I'd gotten that when the twins were born. Now it was up to me.

❧

WE LEFT AFTER lunch. As planned, we swapped Noah for Reese. Telling Reese he was being taken along as bait had been my job, and not one I'd enjoyed.

It seemed simple enough. I was asking him to flirt with girls, not brawl with a biker gang. For Reese, though, I think the brawl would have been less painful.

Like I said, Reese comes with baggage. The issue that caused Nick the most consternation, though, was his complete disinterest in dating. When we sent Reese and Noah to the Sorrentinos, Nick didn't quite know what to do with them. Antonio had decided to step back and let Nick take on the role of guardian. It'd been the right move. When I was pregnant, Nick admitted he'd started thinking about a child of his own. Once the twins came along, he realized single fatherhood was not for him. Taking in Noah and Reese had eventually satisfied that parenting instinct. But at first, the only thing Nick felt confident helping them with was girls.

I tease Nick about being a player. He isn't. No woman who dates him is ever under the illusion that she has him to herself. He's had exclusive relationships, but they're definitely the exception. If a woman hopes to change that, then chances are she won't even get into his bed, because by his age, he's developed a razor-sharp sixth sense for women who say they're good with sex and friendship when they're really hoping for a wedding ring—or at least a set of house keys.

I remember when Reese first went to live with them. Nick had gone through his little black book, looking for a woman with younger sisters, nieces, etc. Because, really, what better way to welcome a young guy and take his mind off his maimed hand? There were parties and double-dates in those early days, when Reese wasn't comfortable refusing. But Nick figured out fast that the dates weren't leading to hook-ups or even second dates. I knew why—his parents had died because Reese fell in love with the wrong girl. Nick didn't know that, but I'd convinced him to respect Reese's decision and be patient with him, even if he did worry that prolonged celibacy really couldn't be good for the young werewolf's health.

So asking Reese to flirt with girls was not as easy as it sounded. But I did it because part of being an Alpha is giving orders you know your Pack won't like. While you can respect their issues, and help them work past them, you can't let those issues get in the way of their Pack responsibilities. ⌒

Fourteen

INDING LORI WAS less of a problem than we expected. She was at the Tim Hortons with her friends again. I sent Reese in ahead of us. Clay and I circled the block, then followed. We weren't averse to her knowing Reese was with us, but we didn't want to advertise it either.

When we got into the coffee shop, Reese was standing beside the girls' table. He'd bought a coffee and stopped to ask them something—recommendations for a bar, it sounded like. He was playing it cool, takeout coffee in hand, looking ready to leave once the conversation ended, but I could already tell they had no intention of letting him get away that quickly. They'd known every guy in town from birth, and now here was a cute blond Aussie. By the time we'd bought our coffee, they'd persuaded him to take a seat.

We took a table across the shop. The noise level—lots of patrons calling out holiday wishes and chattering away—meant we couldn't hear Reese, but that was intentional. If I could listen in, I would, and they might figure out we were eavesdropping. Better to trust Reese.

We'd barely taken our seats when I noticed a girl watching us. Watching me, not Clay, which was good, because she looked about fourteen. All it took from me was a smile, and she zipped over.

"Are you the reporter?" she asked. "The one writing about the wolves?"

"I am." I gestured to the empty seat beside me.

She didn't sit, just stood there, clutching a hot chocolate.

I waited a beat, then said, "Are you interested in wolves?" It was a decent bet. She was too young to have been at the party. Well, no—that's the mother in me, who'd like to think fourteen-year-olds wouldn't party with college-aged kids. But this one didn't look like the type.

She sat quickly and blurted, "I think it was wolves that killed and…" She swallowed. "Everyone says the wolves don't come down here, but my little sister saw one. Right in the woods behind our house."

"A wolf?"

She nodded. "A black one."

That had Clay's head snapping up. "Black?"

"There is such a thing," she said, chin lifting. "I looked it up. Eastern wolves are never black, but gray wolves can be." She hesitated, then added, "It might not have been a full wolf, though. She said it had blue eyes and it was really big."

Shit.

"When did this happen?" I asked.

"In September. Before my stepdad came for Peyton— that's my sister."

Peyton. The little girl who'd gone missing. And she'd seen what seemed to be one of the Eatons in wolf form shortly before she disappeared?

"Your sister," I said. "Have you heard from her?"

"Oh, sure. Her and my stepdad call every week. They're hoping to come up for Christmas, maybe New Year's. My mom and my stepdad are still working out custody stuff, but I think Mom's okay with Peyton staying with him."

The girl was definitely with her father, then. I exhaled in relief. Yet if the Eatons were getting that close to children while in wolf form, that was a problem. A big problem.

I talked to the girl, and made notes, so I'd seem to be taking her story seriously. While we chatted, I noticed someone who seemed to be waiting his turn to speak to me. A bearded man in a plaid jacket. I smiled and nodded, acknowledging him. I didn't rush the girl, but I didn't prolong the conversation either. When she was ready to go, I thanked her for her information and gave her my email address.

She'd barely vacated her chair before the bearded man slid into it. He nodded to Clay first.

"I'm Bobby Walters," he said. "I hear Doc Woolcott talked to you about the Mitchell boy."

The man's name sounded familiar, but I wasn't sure why until he said, "My dogs didn't eat that boy. I know the doc thinks they did and I'm sure that's what he told you, but they didn't."

"Okay."

He leaned forward, as if waiting for me to challenge him. When I didn't, he pulled back and ran his tongue over his wind-chapped lips.

"They didn't," he said. "When I went out that morning, they were all in the pen. They were all hungry. None of them got out. I'm real careful about that, because they did escape a few times after I built the new kennel. There's bear in these woods and damned fool city hunters who don't know a wolf from a husky. I gotta look after my dogs. I can't let them get out. I've taken care of that."

"Okay."

"You don't believe me."

I looked at him. "I'm not from the SPCA. I'm not from an animal rights group. I'm not trying to blame anyone for what happened. I'm just gathering data for an article that covers over a dozen incidents like this. If I find that wolves seemed responsible, that's okay. If it seems to be dogs, that's okay, too. It's all just data. Even if you told me your dogs did it, I wouldn't report that to anyone. It's not my concern."

"They didn't do it."

"Okay."

"They were in the kennel all night."

"Okay."

He stayed for another minute, and I realized he wanted me to argue, because he wanted the chance to defend himself and his dogs. Not to me, but to everyone sitting around us, listening in. People blamed his dogs and he knew it. When I wouldn't argue—and Clay didn't say a word—there was nothing he could do but leave.

As Walters was going, Reese got my attention. He motioned he was done. I nodded, and gestured discreetly to let us leave first.

We got out the door, and saw a familiar face heading our way—Douglas Eaton, shoulders hunched against the cold, no coat on, walking fast, Tim Hortons debit card in his hand.

When he saw us, I expected him to decide he really didn't need that caffeine hit after all. He did glance behind him, but only to look at Walters, now climbing into his truck. Walters waved and shouted something about poker. Eaton replied. Once Walters had driven off, Eaton sped up again until he reached us.

"Morning." He managed a smile for me. "Getting your Timmy's?"

"I was."

"You're Canadian, right? I mean, I'd heard that." A spark of panic, his gaze shooting to Clay. "Not that I was prying—"

"It's not a secret," I said. "I grew up in southwestern Ontario. Went to U of T. So, yes—" I lifted my almost empty cup. "—getting my Timmy's. Not a double-double, though."

A nod and a more genuine smile at that, but still cautious. "I, uh, see Bobby was in there. He's the guy I mentioned to your friend. With the sled dogs." He glanced over his shoulder, making sure no one else was close enough to overhear, then lowered his voice. "He was telling you his dogs didn't eat that boy, wasn't he?"

"He was."

Eaton shifted his weight. "Well...I'm not sure I'd pay much attention to that. They do get out. Yes, I know you think I'm going to say that since you suspect my brother or I did it, but I'd appreciate it if you'd take a hard look at Bobby's dogs. Check the police reports, Woolcott's report, talk to the guys at the scene."

"We will."

"Okay. Thanks. I—"

"Doug?" The voice called out from behind us.

We turned to see Reese striding toward us, a pained look on his face. It wasn't him who'd hailed Eaton, though. That would be the person who was likely the cause of Reese's expression. Lori Romero, hurrying along beside him faster than her high-heel boots should have allowed on the icy sidewalk.

"Did you get my message?" Lori said to Eaton as they reached us.

"Yeah, sorry, Lori. Things have just been busy. I'm sorry Mark isn't calling you back, but…" He shrugged. "I'm just his brother."

She nodded and seemed ready to hurry after her prey, only to realize Reese had stopped, too. Eaton greeted him—they met yesterday at the chalet.

Eaton turned back to Lori. "About Mark. I'm real sorry, hon, but if he's not returning your calls, you might want to forget him. He's got a girlfriend in North Bay. I know they've been having trouble and he probably didn't mention her, but I think they're back together."

"Oh." Her eyes widened, gaze shooting to Reese, mortified. "Mark and I weren't—We're just friends. I was worried because he said he'd drive me to Toronto tomorrow for last-minute Christmas shopping."

"Well, he must have forgotten, because he's gone back to North Bay and—"

He was interrupted as a snow-covered minivan slowed beside us. A middle-aged woman in the passenger seat called out. "Lori?"

"Hey, Mom," Lori said. "I'm sorry. I was just heading home. I got caught up talking to the girls at Tim's."

Her mother's gaze shot to Reese, and she said dryly, "I see."

"Mommy!" shouted a voice from the back seat. "I saw Santa, Mommy!"

The man in the driver's seat put down the rear window, and I saw a little girl about Kate's age bouncing in her booster seat, lips cherry-red from the candy-cane clutched in her hand.

"I saw Santa, Mommy!"

I realized she was talking to Lori. The young woman stepped to the window and leaned in to kiss her, then pretended to bite the candy cane. The girl shrieked and pulled it back.

Lori turned to Reese. "This is my daughter, Patsy."

There was a note of defiance in her voice.

I said hi, and asked the little girl about the Santa visit. She chattered for a minute, then her grandmother said, "We'd better let the nice people go, Patsy. Poor Mr. Eaton is freezing. Where's your jacket, Doug?"

She chided him when he admitted he'd left it in the drugstore. The little girl waved at him and said something about candy canes. Eaton replied, but seemed…Nervous? He promised her one next time she came by, but stayed on the sidewalk, not having joined us at the minivan window.

"Lori?" her dad said. "Can we give you a ride home? Your mom has her optometrist appointment at three and—"

"You need to drive her because of the eye drops. I know. Sorry." She turned to Reese and whispered, "Text me," then opened the minivan door and climbed in.

When they were gone, Eaton said, "I should leave, too. Just one more thing I meant to mention. I don't know how far you guys run, but you should steer clear of the bog to the northeast. It looks frozen, but it's not. Nearly fell in a sinkhole out there a week ago."

"Steer clear of the bog," I said.

"Right."

He said his goodbyes and we parted. When we were back at the truck, I said, "If Eaton is hiding his brother, I think we have a pretty good idea where he is."

"Northeast of our cabin," Clay said, and climbed into the driver's seat. "Near the bog." ⌒

Fifteen

THE EVENTS OF the last couple of hours had only reinforced what I'd already suspected. Mark Eaton killed Dillon Mitchell. His brother knew. When we arrived in town, Eaton thought we'd come for Mark, and squirreled him away. Now he was madly trying to cover his tracks. Convince us his brother had gone on a walkabout in the woods and couldn't be reached. Blame local sled dogs for the scavenging. Suggest to his brother's girlfriend that his lack of contact only meant he was no longer interested.

Mark Eaton had been at the party. When Reese was talking to the girls, he'd mentioned the tragedy and Lori's friends filled him in. Lori had tried to convince Reese she was not a grief-stricken girlfriend, by admitting she and Dillon had already broken up, and she'd been at the party with a "male friend" to convince him that the relationship was over. The friend, Reese confirmed, was Mark Eaton.

Lori's friends thought Reese looked like a sweet hook-up, too, and the bonds of friendship only stretch so far. So, they'd hinted Mark was more than a friend and mentioned a fight between the two guys.

As for what happened after that, the general consensus seemed to be that Mark and Lori immediately took off, and spent the night at his brother' place. Lori hotly denied it. She said they'd stayed at the party after Dillon left, then Mark drove her home.

Did Mark follow Dillon out and kill him? Did he drive Lori home and come back to hide his crime by scavenging the remains? Or did Lori *and* Mark follow Dillon out? Did Dillon die accidentally, and Mark returned to cover it up?

I wasn't happy with any of those scenarios. There was a piece missing here, but we weren't finding it until we found Mark Eaton.

*

LOCATING THE BOG took some effort. After consulting maps and the Internet and finding nothing conclusive, I had Clay ask at a gas station. Turned out the kid manning the pumps was an avid snowmobiler. He knew exactly what we were looking for. When we said we'd been warned to avoid it, he seemed perplexed.

"It's frozen," he said. "If I can ride my sled there, it's safe for you guys to walk on, and it's a great place if you're looking for wildlife. Some folks around here get funny about visitors. Act like the forest belongs to them. It's public land. You want to hike, go ahead. Just be careful. Cell phones don't work out there. You get lost, you'll be walking awhile before you pick up a signal."

*

"WHEN DID YOU last Change?" I asked Reese as we tramped into the woods.

"Two nights ago." He kicked aside a length of vine before we tripped over it. "You're going to Change to track this guy, right?"

"We are."

"So will I, if you need me—"

"If Elena needs you to Change, you will," Clay cut in. "Doesn't matter if you did it a week ago or ten minutes ago."

"I know that. I just meant…" He caught Clay's look and gave a soft growl of frustration. They held each other's gazes before Reese dropped first.

It probably seemed like a small thing to Reese. A matter of semantics. But when the Pack is so small and so tight-knit, it's very easy to let lines blur in the field.

"Let me rephrase that," Reese said. "If you were going to give me the option of a pass, Elena, I don't need it."

"Maybe, but if you don't have to Change, it'll take you longer. You can follow on foot. We'll call when we find Mark Eaton. You can make sure he doesn't bolt while we're Changing back."

"And you can carry our clothing," Clay said.

CLAY FOUND US thick pockets of bush that allowed privacy. Werewolves rarely Change communally. It's like going to the bathroom. You don't want anyone watching you do it. Clay, of course, doesn't see the hang-up, but this is one case where Jeremy has insisted he learn to respect our idiosyncrasies. A werewolf that's uncomfortable is a werewolf that can't Change.

Speaking of uncomfortable...

At Stonehaven, we have a special spot for winter Changes, sheltered from the wind, with a raised platform and cubbies for our clothing. No such luxury here. My clothing hung from bushes, rings and watch zipped in a coat pocket, as I knelt naked in the snow and tried to convince my body, once again, that it's possible to completely change its structure. Even after twenty years, my body refuses to be convinced, and it declares that skepticism with that kind of pain unknown by anyone who hasn't given drug-free birth to twins.

As usual, Clay was finished first. My excuse is that he has another twenty years' experience on me. I tell myself that means it hurts less, meaning it'll hurt less for me one day, too, but I suspect that's not true. He's just less of a wuss about the "Oh God, kill me now" agony.

He was out and circling my thicket while I still lay belly down in the snow, panting. Once he was sure I was at the recovery stage—and therefore unlikely to add to his scar tissue if he interrupted—he stuck his muzzle in and prodded my flank. I growled, fangs bared, a warning against impatience. When I found the energy, I opened my eyes.

He stood in front of me, a two-hundred pound golden wolf with bright blue eyes. Our hair color translates into fur color and our eyes stay the same, as does our mass. Otherwise, we're all wolf.

Clay lowered his nose and touched it to mine. A gentle, loving gesture to his exhausted mate. Promptly followed by chomping the nape of my neck and swinging me out of the thicket into a snowdrift, then dancing away before I could retaliate.

I did retaliate, of course. I just had to catch him first. We play-wrestled for a few minutes. My last two Changes had been alone at Stonehaven while Clay had been gone. Changing alone is like dining out alone. It satisfies the physical hunger, but it's awkward and lonely and otherwise completely unsatisfying. Clay and I had reunited as humans two days ago. This was our wolf reunion, and just as important.

It was only when we finished that Reese came to collect our clothing. He'd been less than fifty feet away, sitting on a log, guarding us as we Changed. I'm sure he'd seen us goofing around, but he stayed where he was until Clay ran over. I hung back. There's something uncomfortable about being in wolf form around a Pack mate who's still human. I'm fine if it's Clay, but even that took years. My issue. I'll get over it someday. Or I won't.

I'd told Reese he could follow us, but the key word there was "could." He could attempt it and he had my permission to do so. Physically being able to follow, though, was an impossibility. We took off, loping over the snow, moving fast enough that our paws didn't break the crust, leaving him to trudge along, falling farther behind.

As we ran, Clay kept his nose up, sampling the air, searching for human scents. We'd Changed south of the bog and the wind was coming from the north, which put us in perfect position to catch a scent. But we had a better plan than that. If Doug Eaton was keeping Mark out here, he had to visit him. That meant driving, parking and walking. There might be a road to the north of the bog, but that would be a longer drive along difficult roads. If he parked, it made sense he'd do it on the road we'd come in on, so we were running west, roughly parallel to that road as I kept my nose down and searched the ground for Eaton's trail. I could pick up hints of scent, but they were old hiker and hunter trails buried by snow.

We were all the way to the other side of the bog before I finally hit Doug Eaton's trail. It was right on top of the snow— big boot marks where he'd tramped through in the past day.

After that, following his trail was easy. He made no attempt to cover his tracks. Probably figured in all these miles of wilderness, we'd never find it. Besides, he'd warned us away from the bog.

Yet the fact that he'd warned us off meant we *didn't* race pell-mell down the trail. In fact, we slowed so much that Reese caught up. I motioned for him to scan the surrounding woods as we walked. Why? Because we could be stepping into a trap.

Still, I doubted it. Eaton knew Reese was with us, meaning he and his brother would be facing at least three Pack wolves. It was exactly the kind of arrogant, macho, brain-dead move I'd expect from a lot of mutts. But Eaton seemed neither arrogant, macho or brain-dead. What he did seem to be was naive. Living up here, away from other werewolves, he had no experience covering his crimes—and it wasn't his he was covering. He'd gotten worried and came up with what probably seemed a perfectly plausible excuse to keep us away from the bog.

As I expected, no one leaped out at us. Eventually we found the cabin. More of a shack really—a weathered wood building meant for shelter and nothing more.

There were no windows on this side and the wind was coming toward us, but we still kept our distance. We scouted in a wide semi-circle. Turned out there were no windows at all. When the wind hit, though, it went right through the old shack and carried a fresh scent out to us. Mark Eaton. Just Mark.

Reese motioned that he'd circle again. I nodded, then nudged Clay toward a patch of brush to begin his Change. Less than ten minutes passed. Then he stepped, naked, from the thicket.

"Any sign of—?" he began.

A blast of bitter, sub-zero wind whipped past.

"Holy shit! Okay, *that's* cold."

I gave a growling chuckle and nudged him back into the thicket. He grabbed handfuls of my fur, yanked me onto his lap and huddled against me.

When I grumbled, he said, "You make me Change, you gotta keep me warm."

I chuffed and gave him a look.

"Yeah, you're Alpha-elect, so you're the one giving the orders, but as the commander, it's your job to keep the lowly foot-soldiers from freezing to death."

He pulled me up so I was sitting on his lap, then buried his face in the fur around my neck. For Clay, there is no disparity between forms. Two halves of the whole. He could huddle here with me and talk to me as if I was in human form. It's me, either way. Of course, there is one area of our lives where he does mark a distinction between the wolf me and the human me, and never the twain shall be confused, for which I am very grateful. I can adjust to a lot, but that would be taking unification of form a step—hell, a few miles—too far.

Moments later, I smelled Reese. He should be able to smell us downwind when he got closer, but with a young werewolf, it's never a guarantee. When I tried leaving the thicket to guide him, Clay tightened his grip and kept me firmly on his lap.

Reese stopped outside the brush and tried blindly pushing clothing in.

"I'm decent," Clay said. "And even if I wasn't, it's nothing you haven't seen before."

"Right. I just thought Elena might be—"

"She's not."

Reese stuck his head in. "Ah. She made you Change back while she keeps her fur coat. Smart."

"Sadistic," Clay said.

He took his clothing and finally let me get up. I went out and waited. A minute later, Clay followed.

I told them to leave my clothing and go on to the cabin. Actually, "told them" is a bit of an exaggeration. Giving orders in wolf form is a test of any Alpha's communication abilities. I suppose we could learn some more sophisticated form, but if I ever suggested we develop a code, I'd be laughed out of the Pack. Like wolves, werewolves have gotten by just fine without speech for millennia.

The Change wasn't faster, but when I finished, it was too damned cold to lie down and give myself time to recover. I yanked on my clothes and headed out.

The guys were at the cabin. I hadn't told them not to go in, but Clay understood that was a given. While Jeremy rarely joined us in the field, I wanted in on everything.

I let Clay take the door. He waited for my signal, then threw his shoulder against it. The door flew clear off its hinges and he charged inside. We followed, flanking his rear.

Sixteen

*I*NSIDE, WE FOUND a mattress on the floor, and Mark Eaton on the mattress, sound asleep. Clay grabbed him by the back of his jacket and yanked him into the air. Only then did he wake, all four limbs shooting out.

"Wh-what—?"

He stopped. He went still. He twisted to look back at Clay and his nostrils flared.

"You're—"

Clay threw him onto the mattress. He scrambled up, blinking madly, shaking his head as if to clear it.

"You— I—" More blinking as he swallowed. He made a face. Drugged. So he wasn't hiding here willingly. Eaton must have decided drugs were safer than ropes. Or more humane.

"Do you know who we are?" I asked.

He jumped at the sound of my voice. I stepped forward. He stared at me. Openly gawked. Not an uncommon reaction. From werewolves, that is—I've never been "open-mouthed gape" material otherwise. I'd be the first female of his species he's ever seen. More importantly, the first he's ever smelled. Apparently there's some scent I give off, some combination of pheromones that makes the guys—or at least their bodies— say "hot damn."

Most handle it badly. We're talking about men accustomed to letting their bodies take charge, and their brains trail behind. Some just flirt. Some attempt displays of male braggadocio rarely seen outside bars in New Jersey. Some launch straight into caveman "jump me" mode, only to learn that, while I may be female, I'm still a werewolf.

Smart ones act like Reese had when he first met me—after that first shock of physical reaction, he couldn't put enough distance between us. The other night, when Eaton stopped by, he'd made damn sure he stayed back and didn't look my way, not with Clay standing right there. Again, smart.

The feeling would pass as they got used to me. It was only those first encounters that were troublesome.

So when Mark Eaton gaped at me, I thought we were going to have a problem. But he only gawked, the way you might if you saw a zebra strolling in downtown Toronto.

"She asked a question," Clay said. "You'll answer her. Now."

"Right. I know who you are and what you're doing here. You're investigating the death of Dillon Mitchell, and my brother has convinced you I did it."

"Convinced us?"

Mark waved at the shack. "He knows that by holding me here, he's convincing you that either I've bolted or he's hiding me from you. He's pulling his submissive routine, isn't he?"

We said nothing.

"I'm sure he is. Acting all nervous, convincing you he's protecting me. Going out of his way to persuade you it wasn't me, while nailing the holes in my coffin with…"

He blinked more, as if still struggling to focus.

"Are you saying your brother killed Dillon Mitchell?" I asked.

"No, Doug isn't a man-eater. I don't know how that boy died, but it wasn't Doug." He paused. "Unless Dillon knew something and Doug killed him for that. I don't think he'd eat him, but—" A lip-curl of distaste. "I guess he might, if he was trying to cover it up." He nodded. "You know, that might be it. Doug kills Dillon, trying to make it look natural. Except that it brings you guys running, so he has another reason to lock me up."

"*Another* reason?"

"He wants—" His head shot up. He looked from me to Clay to Reese. "If you guys are here, where are your kids?"

"What?"

"Your kids. Your little girl. Who's looking after her?"

"Why?"

"That's what he's after. That's why he locked me up here. So I couldn't warn you. He saw your little girl and—"

I wheeled on Clay. Before he could speak, I had the keys from his pocket and was running for the door, pushing Reese in front of me, calling for Clay to bring Mark.

Mark didn't need to finish. I knew exactly what Doug Eaton had seen when he looked at Kate. The same thing foster fathers and brothers had seen when they looked at me, all those years ago.

Prey.

*

I WANTED TO drive. But this was one time where the chain of command didn't apply. When I tried getting into the driver's seat, Clay picked me up and dumped me on the passenger's side. He was right. My heart was thumping so hard I could barely breathe.

I called Nick's cell again. My fingers shook so much that if I'd had to do more than hit redial, I doubt I'd have managed it. But, like the half-dozen times I'd tried while we were racing to the truck, there was no signal.

In the back seat, Reese was doing the same, trying Noah's number. Mark sat beside him, silent.

"Still out of range," Reese said. "But they're okay. Nick's with them and he—"

"She knows," Clay said.

I knew Reese just wanted to reassure me that the twins were safe with Nick. But right now, I probably wouldn't relax if the entire Pack was with them.

I turned to Mark. "Tell us about your brother."

I hoped to hear something to convince me that I'd misunderstood or he'd misinterpreted. But Mark's story was exactly what I expected.

Growing up, Douglas Eaton had always been awkward around girls his own age. He dated, but he seemed to be performing a duty. Mark had decided his older brother was gay. He knew their father wouldn't be able to handle it, so he went along with Eaton's charade and didn't push him toward women.

Then came the night, a few months ago, when Mark showed up unexpectedly and found his brother home with little Peyton James.

"He'd lured her into the woods in wolf form," he said. "He got her lost, then Changed back and 'rescued' her. When I got there, he hadn't done anything yet. He was just...staring at her." Mark shuddered at the memory. "I took one look at his face and I knew I'd made a huge mistake about my brother. If I hadn't shown up that night…" He took a deep breath. "Maybe he wouldn't have done anything. Maybe he was still working up to it. Or maybe he'd been working up to it for years, with other girls, and if I hadn't come by…"

He went on to explain that he'd persuaded Eaton to relinquish the girl. Except they couldn't just let her leave. Mark didn't trust his brother not to do the same thing again. He had to remove temptation. Eaton knew Peyton's father and knew he wanted custody, so Mark persuaded him to call and say he'd found Peyton wandering the woods and he thought her dad needed to take her before her mother's neglect led to tragedy.

Things seemed to improve after that. There were no more incidents, and when Mark suggested moving in, Eaton seemed happy. He even introduced Mark to Lori Romero.

"Who just happens to have a little girl," I said.

Mark nodded. "I didn't know at first. She's only twenty, so I never suspected that. Then I found out. I broke it off with Lori the night of the party. Doug didn't like that. We've been arguing ever since. Then we were in town the other day and smelled you. Doug saw your daughter and… And I knew we were in trouble. Big trouble. Maybe he could control himself with human girls. But a werewolf?" He shook his head.

Mark had tried to sneak over and warn us. His brother caught him. They fought. An argument turned to blows. Mark ended up with cracked ribs, a possible concussion and a broken ankle. He'd woken to find himself drugged and dumped in the cabin. He'd tried to escape yesterday, but only made it a few hundred feet on his injured foot before collapsing. His brother had found him. He'd told him we were on the trail of a man-eater and suspected him. If Mark tried to escape again, Eaton would tell us where to find him.

"Got a signal!" Reese said. "And Noah's phone's ringing. It's…going to voicemail."

"Leave a message," I said as I dialed Nick's phone. It blipped out the first time, but worked the second. It rang. Rang. Rang.

"You're reached the voicemail of Nick Sorr—"

I hung up and tried again.

✒

I LEFT A message for Nick. There was nothing else to do.

Nick wasn't the best fighter in the Pack. He wasn't the smartest guy in the Pack. But he was the most loyal. If we asked him to look after our kids, that's what he'd do and that's all he'd do until we returned. If Eaton struck, then it wouldn't matter that Nick wasn't the strongest or smartest in the Pack. That was like saying a second-string major league player wasn't good at baseball—he was still heads and shoulders above any amateur. Nick could take on Eaton. No question.

The real issue? I was furious with myself. Eaton was a pedophile. I was a sexual-abuse survivor. How the hell hadn't I figured it out? I'd seen him around Kate. I'd seen him around Lori Romero's little girl. In both cases, he'd seemed anxious. I'd noticed that, but somehow it hadn't pinged my radar. Maybe I had no radar at all, and I'd been fooling myself that I did, and I'd let my daughter slip into the sphere of a predator because of it. ⁓

Seventeen

I WAS OUT OF the truck as soon as it slowed. Reese was, too, and he beat me to the front door. The first tug told me it was locked, but before I could push him out of the way, he slammed his shoulder into it and the door flew open. Then he stepped aside and let me through.

The house was empty. I ran to the back door and found all the coats and boots missing.

"They've gone out for a walk," I said as Clay brought Mark through.

"You have to find them," Mark said. "Doug's been watching the house, waiting for you to take her out so he can lure her off, like he did with the James girl."

Before he finished, I was out the back door. Reese and I took off at a run, and I made it to the forest's edge before I realized Clay wasn't with us. I looked back. He had Mark, arm around him to keep him upright as he limped along.

I knew babysitting a wounded mutt was not what Clay wanted to do right now. He said nothing, though. Sticking to his assignment until I said otherwise.

I glanced at Reese. I could tell him to watch Mark, but that meant one less person hunting.

"Leave him," I said to Clay.

"No, I can help." Mark pushed off from Clay's support. A few faltering steps, then he stumbled.

"Stay there," I said. "Right there."

❧

MARK WAS RIGHT. His brother was in the forest. I picked up his scent on the wind right away.

I'd screwed up. It wasn't just that I hadn't recognized what Eaton was. I'd left my children vulnerable in another way—by not telling them what *we* were.

I'd left them unprepared to deal with a werewolf threat. Not just a pedophile, but any mutt who decided to target them. If they knew, then we could teach them how to distinguish a werewolf scent, something Kate seemed to have already figured out. Simply telling them to avoid strangers wasn't enough.

Eaton had lured Peyton James away from her house using his wolf form. Could he do that with Kate? Of course he could.

Because, then, he wasn't a stranger. He wasn't a man. He was a wolf, a creature that fascinated her, even if she didn't understand why, and if she saw one, she'd follow, because I hadn't prepared her to do otherwise.

"Can you smell him?" I asked Clay as we ran along the path from the chalet.

"Eaton?" He lifted his nose to the wind and inhaled. He nodded grimly.

"Reese? Can you?"

He was trying, but finally he said, "No. Sorry. But I can smell Nick, Noah and the kids on this path. I can follow if you two want to go after—"

"No. Clay?"

"On it."

He veered northwest. My cell phone rang. As I fumbled it from my pocket, Clay didn't stop, just looked back, anxiety flashing in his eyes. I waved for him to wait.

"Just got your message," Nick said in greeting. "Damned jacket's so thick I didn't hear it ring. The message was garbled, too. Something about Eaton and Kate?"

"Where are the kids?"

"Right here. We're playing hide-and-seek."

"Hide—?" My voice squeaked with panic.

"Um, yes. I can hear them and find them by scent, Elena. Not exactly a fair game, but it's safe."

"Right. Sorry. Could you please—?"

"Noah?" He called. "Find the kids." Then, to me. "We'll round them up and take them back to the cottage. Trouble, I'm guessing?"

"Eaton's out here. Possibly in wolf form. He's after Kate."

"Kate? Why—?" Only a brief pause. Then he swore. In some things, he catches on faster than anyone else. He understands things better, too, and I didn't have to say another word. He knew exactly how freaked out I'd be. He signed off with an abrupt promise that he'd find Kate and get her to safety.

CLAY TOOK OFF after Eaton. Reese and I raced to where I could now hear Noah's voice.

"Kate!" he called. Then, "She was right there. I could hear—"

Nick's whisper, shushing him before Eaton overheard. I ran full out, branches lashing me, heart pounding. I could hear Reese behind me, whispering, "It's okay. Nick's got them. It's okay," and part of me wanted to whip around and tell him to shut up, just shut up, it wasn't okay. But I heard the anxiety in his voice and felt him, right there on my heels, and I knew we were lucky to have him, damned lucky, and I had to hold it together, be the kind of Alpha he expected. The kind they all expected.

A figure moved in the trees. Downwind, so I couldn't catch the scent and the forest was so thick that all I saw was a figure and a flash of a parka and dark hair.

Eaton.

I held up my hand, stopping Reese before he plowed into me. Eaton was just standing there, almost hidden in the trees. Looking east. Watching something. I eased in that direction and saw Kate in her purple snowsuit, doing a very poor job of hiding, as she crouched behind a log. Her hat was askew, blond curls tumbling out, her cheeks rosy from the cold, her blue eyes dancing. My beautiful little girl. And Eaton stood there, less than fifty feet away—

He shifted, and I sucked in breath so fast I nearly choked.

It wasn't Douglas Eaton watching Kate. It was Mark.

"Damn it," Reese whispered, relieved. "Moron couldn't stay put." He started forward.

I grabbed Reese's arm as I stared, transfixed, at Mark Eaton. I watched him watching my daughter, and the look in his eye hit me like a punch to the gut, and I knew what had been missing when Douglas Eaton was around Kate and Lori Romero's daughter. This look. The one that brought a thousand memories spilling back, and a whimper bubbling up in

KELLEY ARMSTRONG

my gut, silenced by a wave of fury. I launched myself at Mark, barely hearing Reese's exclamation of surprise.

Mark *did* hear Reese and he turned, saw me and ran toward Kate, his ankle obviously fine. He was closer, but I was running as fast as I could and—

My foot caught on a vine. I stumbled. Reese grabbed me and I recovered fast, but it was enough to give Mark the advantage he needed.

"Kate!" I shouted.

She looked up and grinned. Then she saw my face and turned, as if sensing Mark. Seeing him, she jumped up. She started to run to me, but he was almost to her and—

A shape dropped from the trees and landed on Mark's back, knocking him down. Mark reared up. He grabbed Logan and wrenched him off, arm swinging to throw him. I hurled myself at him. Kate did, too. She caught his arm and sank her teeth into his hand. He screamed and dropped Logan. I grabbed Logan and tossed him to Reese, then caught Kate and pulled her off him. She didn't let go and when I pulled her away, she took a chunk of his hand with her. Blood spattered the snow as Mark yowled.

He charged us. I wrapped my arms around Kate and backed away, stumbling and tripping, but I couldn't put her down, not even to fight him, couldn't let her go. He pounced. I kicked and hit his shin and he fell back, but he only snarled

174

and shook himself off and came at us again. Reese hesitated, Logan in his arms, looking to me for direction. I shook my head, telling him not to let go of Logan.

A shout from the east. Nick racing at us, Noah right behind. Mark ignored them and charged again. I dove, shielding Kate. As I fell, a blur shot from the trees to the west. Clay barreled into Mark's side and sent him flying. Then he fell on him. Mark hit him with everything he had, fists and feet and even teeth, snapping and snarling as if he was in wolf form, instinct taking over.

Clay glanced at me. I nodded. Then I hoisted Kate up, her face pressed against my chest and motioned for Nick to take Logan from Reese. We hustled the children away from the fight. Reese stayed and when I glanced back, he was circling with Noah, waiting for Mark to make a run for it. He wouldn't try. Clay wasn't fighting hard. Not yet. Just keeping things going until we got the kids far enough away. When we did, I heard an unmistakable snap as Clay broke Mark Eaton's neck.

The crackle of bush to my left. I looked over to see Douglas Eaton, in human form, jogging through the woods. He saw me and stopped. I tensed, but he kept his distance. He looked at me, then at Nick, both of us clutching a child to our chest. His gaze swung behind us and I looked over my shoulder to see what he did—Clay standing over Mark, the boys at his back.

"He came after our daughter," I said.

Eaton's head dipped, his gaze unable to meet mine. "I'm sorry. I tried…I didn't know what to do."

I nodded, hugged Kate tighter and headed back for the house as Eaton walked to where his brother lay dead in the snow. ⌒

Eighteen

THE KIDS WERE fine. At first, I wasn't sure how much they understood, but as I cleaned Mark Eaton's blood from Kate's face, she said, "That man wanted to hurt me."

I hesitated, and the mother in me wanted to say, "No, everything is fine, it was just a mistake." The Alpha in me knew I couldn't. Whether my children were werewolves or not, they were part of the Pack and they needed to understand the dangers.

"Yes," I said. "He did."

"Logan saved me."

She looked at her brother, standing beside the sink, watching with quiet concern, and she smiled. He mumbled something and dropped his gaze, but his eyes glowed.

"He did," I said.

"You and Daddy helped," she added. "I did a little, too. But it was mostly Logan."

"It was." I bent and picked him up in a hug so tight he squirmed until I put him down again.

"It was just lucky," Logan said. "We were trying to trick Uncle Nick and Noah. Kate was only pretending to hide. They'd find her and I'd jump out of the tree. Only it wasn't them that found her, so it was an even better plan than we thought."

"It was."

I looked at them, and I thought of what had almost happened and—

"I'm okay, Mommy," Kate said, putting out her arms for a hug. When I bent to embrace her, she whispered. "The blood is scary, but don't worry. It's just his."

I kissed her and blinked back tears, and wet the cloth again.

*

WHEN I'D FINISHED, Nick was waiting outside the door. Clay had brought Eaton to the house to speak to me. When I turned the twins over to Nick, he put an arm around my shoulders and whispered, "We'll talk later."

When it came to my past, I'd learned that Nick made a better confidante. By talking to Clay about it, I was saying, "These people hurt me and I forbid you to do anything about it." He tried to hide his frustration, but I'd come to realize it wasn't fair, and turned instead to the guy who'd just listen and offer me all the support and sympathy I needed—and the kick in the ass when I needed that, too.

I found Clay out back with Reese, Noah and Douglas Eaton. I sent the boys inside to help Nick with the twins, then took Eaton farther from the house where we could talk.

I'm sure he'd already given Clay his story, but Clay had him repeat it to me. The short version was this: take the story Mark had given, reverse the brothers in it and you had something close to the truth.

Growing up, Mark Eaton hadn't taken much interest in girls. Douglas hadn't noticed at first—he was five years older, and off to college before his brother entered high school. When he realized it, he'd suspected his brother was gay and tried to help him deal with that. Mark went along with the ruse.

Soon, though, Eaton noticed his brother's interest in little girls. He saw the way he looked at them, the work and volunteerism he chose bringing him in contact with children. When a girl in their father's neighborhood went missing, Eaton asked Mark if he'd known her. Mark figured out what he was saying. They had a blowout fight, Mark took off, and the girl turned up with her mother, who'd lost custody.

Eaton had apologized and the brothers made up. Then came the night Eaton returned unexpectedly from his girlfriend's place and discovered Mark had gone for a run. He decided to surprise him...and found him at that decrepit cabin with Peyton James. Nothing had happened, but Eaton realized she posed too great a temptation and—thinking of the other case—called her father.

After that, Mark confessed. Lots of sobbing. Lots of self-recrimination. Promises to get help. Vows to stay away from children. Then he started dating Lori Romero. Eaton insisted he break it off. The next morning, Dillon Mitchell was dead after what could have been a werewolf attack, and Mark began a subtle campaign of blackmail. Either Eaton back off about Lori or Mark would frame him as a man-eater. When we showed up, Eaton thought that's exactly what his brother had done. Hence his fear. And when he realized we had a young daughter? Fear escalated to outright panic.

Did Mark fight with Dillon and kill him? Did he eat him? Eaton suspected the death was accidental and Mark took a couple of Bobby Walters's dogs out to eat the body, but I think in spite of everything, he just couldn't bring himself to think his brother was capable of murder and cannibalism. He still loved him.

To keep Mark from Kate, Eaton drugged him and put him in the same cabin where he'd brought Peyton. Then he'd kept coming around us, trying to figure out what to do next. I think he knew something had to be done, that Mark wasn't going to stop, that the next little girl he targeted wouldn't be as lucky as Peyton. Was that why he tipped his hand about the bog? Maybe, subconsciously, yes.

Mark's foot hadn't been injured, as he claimed. Eaton only kept him drugged enough that he couldn't make it to town. Mark had caught our scent as we'd circled outside. He'd called Eaton on the walkie-talkie his brother provided and whispered that we'd come for him and he was in the backseat of our truck heading to our chalet. Eaton had to get over there right away and save him. Eaton fell for it and everything played out as Mark intended, us racing back to the cabin, smelling Eaton in the woods, focusing on him and letting Mark get to Kate.

When it came to Douglas Eaton, I decided to show mercy. I had to call Jeremy to get the official word, but he left the decision up to me. In an ideal world, Eaton would have told us everything from the start. But the reputation of the Pack has endured for centuries, and that reputation says we would have saved ourselves the bother of an investigation and just killed him and his brother. That changed under Jeremy, but it takes more than a generation or two before we can reasonably expect the average mutt to trust us to make a judicious decision.

Eaton had whisked his brother away before he could go after Kate. He'd tried to get to know us a little better, maybe decide if we could be trusted. If that was truly his goal, and I think it was, then we failed. Normally, I'd have listened, but having the twins there made me anxious and defensive. An unfortunate collision of circumstances.

Later I'd talk to Jeremy about what I could have done differently. Maybe nothing.

For now, I sent Reese and Nick to help Douglas Eaton bury his brother in the frozen earth, then we left him alone with his grief.

✦

NICK, REESE AND Noah left the next day. Jeremy had found them a place in Toronto where Antonio would join them, while Jeremy spent Christmas with his girlfriend, Jaime. Then Karl and his wife, Hope, would meet the Pack in Toronto, and they'd all come up on Boxing Day.

Yes, I felt bad about "kicking" the guys out after all their help. But they insisted and Clay insisted, and the next day, when I took the kids to town, we came back to find them gone and our own Christmas began.

And begin it did, at warp speed. Less than twenty-four hours after being attacked by Mark Eaton, the kids were making gingerbread cookies and chattering about Santa and panicking when Clay pretended we'd left their stockings at home. There were no questions about the Eatons or what happened in the forest. Everyone was safe. Christmas was coming. Life moved on.

The guys had left around noon on Christmas Eve, and we crammed those next twelve hours full of everything on the kids' list. By the time the stockings were hung by the chimney with care, Kate and Logan were nestled all snug in front of the fireplace, having literally done that final task, then dropped onto the rug and fallen asleep. We carried them up to bed.

I got the fire going again—the kids had insisted we put it out earlier, so Santa wouldn't get immolated. Clay took off to do something, and I was sitting in front of the blazing fire, munching a cookie left for Santa, when he came into the family room, hair dusted with snow.

"You were outside?" I said.

"Making reindeer tracks."

I lifted my brows.

"Did you hear the kids earlier, talking about reindeer?"

Kate had been concerned that the chalet roof was too steep for the reindeer to touch down on, and Logan insisted they didn't *really* fly.

"That would be magic," he said. "There's no such thing as magic except in books, like Harry Potter. Reindeer can't fly. It's scientifically impossible."

One could argue it was just as impossible for a man to visit every house in the world in one night, but our son is four. He may be scary smart, but he's still four. His logic isn't perfect. But he was certain there was no such thing as flying reindeer.

"So you made reindeer tracks?" I said.

"I did. Not on the roof, of course. That wouldn't work. But they landed in the middle of the yard, then walked over to the house. I figured that should do the trick. I considered adding deer droppings, but Logan would figure out the size differential, so I settled for tracks. Plus a few tufts of deer hair caught in the bushes."

"And you gave our kids flying reindeer."

"I did."

I put my arms around his neck, and wrapped my hands in his damp hair and kissed him. "God, I love you."

He kissed me back, then said, "If I'd known how many brownie points this daddy stuff could win me, I'd have talked you into kids years ago. Would have saved me a lot of trouble."

"It would have."

"Problem is, they're going to grow up." He paused. "We may need to have more."

"We may." I wrapped my hand in his shirtfront and pulled him down in front of the fire.

HIDDEN

WE LAY IN front of the fire, naked, legs entwined as we ate gingerbread cookies and drank hot chocolate from the thermos I'd brought in earlier.

"This feels familiar," he said.

I smiled. "It does."

"Twenty years."

I bit back a sleepy yawn. "Hmm?"

"Twenty years since our first Christmas."

"Twenty? No, it can't be…" I calculated. "Shit. It is."

Twenty years since our first Christmas together. Twenty years since we'd been curled up together on another rug, in another place, munching on gingerbread cookies and sipping hot chocolate.

"The cookies are better," he said. "They actually look like gingerbread men now."

"Because we remembered to buy cookie cutters."

He laughed and we lay there, lost in memories. Then he glanced under the tree.

"I think I see a gift under there for you."

I laughed. "No, you're not going to make me open one early this time."

"One won't hurt." He nudged a small present off a pile with his foot. "There. It fell. Don't make me put it back."

Still grinning, I reached down and scooped it up. It was small and flat, oddly shaped.

"Please don't tell me it's another spare set of keys," I said.

"Mmm, maybe."

I unwrapped it. Inside, I found a silver tree ornament. A circle surrounding a cutout of two wolves on a snowy hill. He'd had it engraved with the years of our first Christmas and this one.

"We're starting a collection," he said. "You'll get one every twenty years. I figure we have three or four more to go." He pursed his lips. "That could mean a lot of kids, to keep me in your good graces."

"You don't need kids for that," I murmured.

I ran my fingers over the wolves. Part of our lives. Such a huge part of our lives. A part that we were keeping from our children.

That, I realized, was the real issue. When our children were old enough to understand, they'd look back on a childhood raised as normal kids, believing their parents were normal people, and they wouldn't see a harmless fantasy, like reindeer tracks in the snow. They'd look back on every part of their lives—on their relationships with the rest of the Pack, on all the times I'd done "research," all the times Clay and I had to leave on "a trip," even on things as small as why they couldn't have pets—and they'd see lies. Lies permeating every aspect of their lives. Every person in their lives telling them lies. Every person they'd trusted to tell them the truth.

We gave them the fantasy of a normal family because that's what I wanted. That's what I'd dreamed of, and as much as I loved my life, there was still part of me that thought "normal" was what my children deserved. But it wasn't. They deserved us—their parents and their extended family—as we really were. They deserved *our* normal.

"I want to tell them," I said.

He didn't ask what I meant, didn't need to, just nodded and said, "Okay."

"Can we talk about that?" I said. "Now? I know it's not the time, but—"

"Now is fine." ⌒

Nineteen

CHRISTMAS MORNING. AWAKE at dawn, the kids tumbling down the stairs, Logan tripping over Kate and sprawling to the floor, Kate helping him up, making sure he was okay before the race resumed. Presents. Not a lot, and not as any statement against commercialism but simply because, let's face it, for our kids, Christmas came year-round, endless toys and books and games from friends and family and, yes, indulgent parents.

Santa gifts first. Then stockings. Then breakfast—pancakes and ham and cookies. Then gifts to each other, still in pajamas, curled up in front of the blazing fire. Afterward, some talk of going outside, but for once, the forest didn't call to anyone, and we were all quite happy to laze about and play board games.

We missed lunch. Hardly shocking, considering breakfast never really ended. At three, the kids realized they'd skipped a meal and insisted on going through the motions of making lunch, even if no one was particularly hungry.

Afterwards, the kids fell asleep by the fire. When they began to stir from their naps, Clay took off. Once the twins were fully awake, they asked where he was.

"He just stepped out," I said, gazing at the window. "He'll be back soon."

"What are you looking for, Mommy?" Kate asked as she climbed onto my lap.

I was about to say "nothing," and slide her back to the floor, then I stopped. Was I ready for this? Really ready?

I took a deep breath, then settled her on my lap, and leaned down to her ear.

"Watch," I whispered.

Logan glanced up from the floor, still sleepy. It took a moment for him to figure out something was going on. When he did, he walked to the window and gazed out.

"What are we looking for?" he asked.

"Just wait."

It only took another minute. Then Clay stepped from the forest in wolf form and my heart jammed into my throat.

I'd wanted to explain it first, sit them down, tell them everything. This had been his idea. What the hell had possessed me to go along with it? How were they supposed to process this? What were they thinking? What was I even going to say?

Clay walked toward the chalet, slowly, his blue eyes fixed on the window. Waiting for me to appear and change my mind, madly wave him away. I wanted to, but I was frozen there, watching him.

He stopped, lowered his head and chuffed, breath streaming from his nostrils. Kate slid from my arms. She walked to the window, pressed her hands to it, her nose to it. Her head tilted one way, then the other as she studied him. Then she turned to me with a blazing grin.

"It's Daddy, isn't it?"

I hesitated, certain I'd misheard. Worry clouded her eyes.

"Mommy? It is, isn't it?"

I nodded. Forced the words out. "It is."

She turned and slugged her brother in the arm. "Told you." She looked at me. "I told him. I saw the werewolves in my book and I said they're real, and he said they weren't."

"You didn't say you thought Dad was..." Logan stared out the window.

Kate took off, shouting that she was going outside, and I didn't think to stop her. I just watched Logan. He didn't step closer to the window. Didn't press against it. There was no smile on his face. He just stared.

I slid from the chair and crouched beside him. "I know this is a big shock, baby."

He kept gazing out the window as Kate now raced over to Clay, plowing through the snow in her slippers, no coat on.

"Is it magic?" Logan asked.

"Yes."

He turned to me. "Can you do that, too? Turn into a wolf?"

I nodded.

"And Jeremy and Uncle Nick and everyone?"

I nodded.

"And me?"

He watched me, his face still expressionless. When I didn't answer, he said, "When I'm older, will I be able to do that?"

"I...we don't know. Maybe."

He grinned then, a grin as bright as his sister's, so sudden it made my breath catch.

"Cool," he said.

He threw his arms around my neck, gave me a quick hug, then raced to the door. Before he ran out, he turned around.

"Can I go—?" he began.

I smiled. "You can."

A second later, the door banged shut. Another second and he was out there, no coat, no boots, wading through the snow to where his sister stood beside Clay, running her hands over his fur. Clay turned. Logan stopped. Clay stepped forward, and looked him in the eyes. Then, slowly, Logan reached out and patted Clay's head and Clay licked his face.

Logan giggled, so loud I could hear him. He wiped his face. Kate pounced on Clay from the back. Logan jumped

him, too, and they went down, shrieking and giggling, rolling in the snow.

I'd done the right thing. Maybe I should have done it sooner. I don't know. Didn't matter. But it was done now and everything was fine.

Kate waved at me through the window. Logan beckoned me out. I smiled, lifted a finger to say I was coming, then headed for the back door to grab their coats and boots and join them. ⌒